D0366618

Acclaim for Daniel Torday's *The Sensualist*

"Daniel Torday has written an altogether new kind of historical fiction: one that filters the legacy of war through two boys' evolving friendship and its tragic unraveling. Torday shows us how these kids are themselves bullied into committing a crime by events that stretch back to Moscow, the labor camps of the Ukraine. The result is an often-hilarious, always powerfully-moving portrait of adolescence as haunted foosball game. With subtlety, humor, and compassion, Torday gives us a coming of age story that is also a record of war's second life, lived by the generation who never experienced war directly, but who proceed through life in its inescapable shadow."

Karen Russell, author of *Swamplandia!*

"Daniel Torday has clearly mastered the acoustics of experience, the mechanics of how the small actions of anyone, of everyone, echo and resonate against the history we all share. With perfectly rendered details of adolescent life in 1990's Baltimore and a large-hearted memory of other times, other places, *The Sensualist* has the rare, unmistakable quality of feeling necessary. A brilliant debut."

Robin Black, author of *If I Loved You, I Would Tell You This*

"I throw at you, without reservation, this adjective: masterful. This book is fast and warm, fraught and intimate—and no slouch in the funny department, either. Daniel Torday's voice is entirely his own. Baltimore is his. Dmitri Zilber is a brilliant character, and I am in love with his sister. I am constantly happy to be in their presence."

Adam Levin, author of *The Instructions*

"In this tenderly told novella, Daniel Torday brings the singular essence of Baltimore vividly to life, and lifts the beating heart of boyhood out of the halls of high school and straight onto the page. But *The Sensualist* does more than that: quietly, carefully, beneath the surface, it charts the arc of a childhood lost, a life irrevocably turned. Dmitri Zilber is a character so strongly imagined he'll fill your own imagination for days; Sam Gerson will draw you close as if to your own childhood friend; and the friendship between the two of them will stay with you long after you set this beautiful book down."

Josh Weil, author of *The New Valley*

"Charting the course of a complicated friendship, Daniel Torday writes beautifully and believably about the agonies, and occasional delights, of late adolescence. This passionate, powerful and shrewdly observed novella packs a massive emotional wallop."

Adrienne Miller, author of *The Coast of Akron*

# THE SENSUALIST
## A NOVELLA BY DANIEL TORDAY

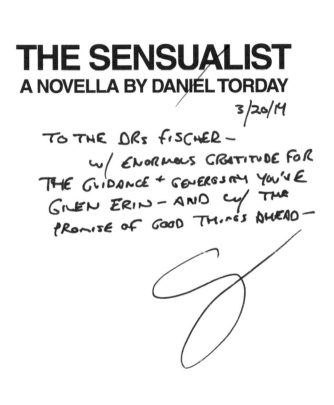

3/20/14

TO THE DRs FISCHER —
    w/ ENORMOUS GRATITUDE FOR
THE GUIDANCE + GENEROSITY YOU'VE
GIVEN ERIN — AND w/ THE
PROMISE OF GOOD THINGS AHEAD —

NOUVELLA

2012

This is a work of fiction. Names, characters, places and incidents are either the product of the author's imagination or are used fictitiously, and any resemblance to actual persons, establishments, events or locales is entirely coincidental.

**THE SENSUALIST**

Copyright Daniel Torday 2012

A Nouvella book / published 2012

Design by Daniel D'Arcy

All rights reserved.

This book, or parts thereof, may not be reproduced in any form without permission.

The scanning, uploading and distribution of this book via the Internet or via any other means without the permission of the publisher is not permitted.

For information go to:
*nouvella.com*

Printed in the United States of America.

*For Erin*

The Sensualist

Baltimore is warm and pleasant. I love it more than I thought—it is so rich in memories—it is nice to look up the street and see the statue of my great uncle and to know that Poe is buried here and that many ancestors of mine have walked in the old town on the bay. I belong here, where everything is civilized and gay and rotted and polite.

F. Scott Fitzgerald, from a letter written at La Paix in 1935

# ONE

The events leading to the beating Dmitri Abramovitch Zilber and his friends would administer to Jeremy Goldstein at the end of my junior year of high school—an act that would make them the talk of every household in Pikesville for months after—started before Dmitri and I even met.

I was sixteen then, and reluctantly finishing my final two years at a high school in Baltimore. At that time I was plagued by an old excoriating Greek gym teacher named Mr. Stephanopoulos. Stephanopoulos was in his early seventies and had taught at that same school for over forty years, and there was no end to the emasculating aphorisms he had developed to remind young men of their insecurity and weakness. He had served for three years in the European Theater, having enlisted when he was seventeen. He took this former bravery and paired it with the paucity of experience he'd accrued in the fifty years since and transformed it into the kind of didacticism only young men in public school are made to endure, and which can only be doled out by hoary old men with war stories no one wants to hear.

I was a moderately talented southpaw pitcher on the school's JV baseball team, and Stephanopoulos was the team coach. He called me into his office on a humid afternoon the last week of my sophomore year and asked me to sit down.

"Gerson," he said. "Your arm looked strong at the end of the season. Fastball has some real pop. I want you as my number two starter next year on the varsity." I did my best to hide my elation as he continued. "But your changeup needs work. Your curveball won't break. You're gonna have to play summer ball, and get out with Mr. Fischer on weekends." Mr. Fischer was the team pitching coach, a silver-haired sauna buddy of Stephanopoulos' and the purported source of a well-traveled rumor that Stephanopoulos had only one testicle, the other one lost during the war, a rumor that mercifully never would be substantiated. "You need to learn to change speeds."

"I want to do that," I said. "But my parents are sending me on a trip to Israel for all of June and July. Maybe I could work with him in August."

Stephanopoulos furrowed his brow—it was substantial, peppered black and white, and it loomed over his rheumy Mediterranean eyes like a dirt-stained snowdrift. "Well, what are you gonna do then, play in the Kosher League?"

He put his eyes back to the line-up card he was filling out and refused to look back up until I'd left his office.

I left the room after hesitating for a second. Pikesville High School was a public school, but in the ghettoized demographics of Baltimore, nine out of every ten of the kids who comprised the student body were Jewish. I had always harbored a suspicion that my teachers were anti-Semites. I had, in fact, developed a strong conjecture that anyone who stood in the way of any of my aims—from my teachers to my parents to the tattooed senior named Leibowitz who sold me Ziploc bags of pot—was an anti-Semite. Faced with the possibility of real anti-Semitism, I was confounded and flattered by the idea that only the insuperable historical accident of my own Judaism might keep me from one day pitching for the Baltimore Orioles.

I didn't officially quit the baseball team that day. Come baseball season, I would simply fail to show up for pre-season training. Over the summer that followed I repeated to anyone who would listen the story of my tacit abdication of the pitching slot.

By the time I returned to school after Labor Day, my insubordination had ossified into an angst-riddled mass. I was the sole whiner in October who refused to go out into the fifty-degree air in only a pair of scabrous, grey nylon-and-polyester school-issued gym shorts. So when Stephanopoulos called out to us on the first wintry day in November and said to suit up for flag-football, my anger had peaked. Stephanopoulos said, "All right, Gerson, go grab us some of those shoulder jobs from the closet"—he meant for me to get the shoulder pads so we could practice in gear, but he referred to everything as a "job"—"so we can get out and play some football."

I stared at my feet.

"What'll it be then, Gerson? Too cold out there for you? You think you're a man, ignoring me? Why don't you pull down your pants so we can see who's a man." This last line was his favorite, along with, on any poor play, "You've only got three brain cells and two are giving the other CPR," and on a dropped ball, "You couldn't catch a cold in a germ factory." I was ready to raise my voice and erupt with two years and one long Middle Eastern summer's worth of anger when Dmitri Zilber, a boy I didn't know, spoke up.

"My father," he said, his words deliberate with the articulation of one who has only just acquired a command of English, "my father says is too cold weather to be running around in shorts. Even in gulag they would not have us playing out in such weather."

I'm not sure if I knew before that day that Dmitri spoke English at all. Stephanopoulos was stunned too. He paused for a second before walking over to Dmitri—the boy stood across the locker room from me—and, pointing his index and middle fingers out straight, Steph poked him hard in the middle of his sternum:

"I doubt your father knows a thing of what happened at a gulag," he said, "and I can damn well guess he hasn't ever played a down of football."

He turned and faced me again, his head not a foot from Dmitri's and said, "Now Gerson, grab some of those goddamn shoulder jobs and flag jobs and a couple of cone jobs and let's get out there."

I'd begun to mope towards the equipment closet when I heard Dmitri say something under his breath. Stephanopoulos barked, "What?"

When Dmitri mumbled back, Stephanopoulos flushed a shade of red only his olive Mediterranean skin could turn. He grabbed Dmitri by the arm and said:

"Get out of here. I don't want to see you again until you've served a suspension." He almost threw Dmitri as he swung him, letting go at the last minute. "I don't care if I ever see your Russian ass again. Get to the principal's office."

I knew next to nothing of this Dmitri Zilber. He had only started at Pikesville the year before. There must have been more than a hundred immigrants from the former Soviet states amongst the twelve hundred students at Pikesville. They were all Jews who had distant relatives in Baltimore and had arrived with some help, offered grants to live under care of family. All we really knew was that these Russians hung out in large groups and rarely talked to us. They were stolid and unapproachable.

Those of us who'd grown up here weren't entirely un-aware of our good fortune. We'd helped our mothers fill Glad bags with our old clothes and brought them to Synagogue on Park Heights Avenue—there were five shuls on the seven-mile stretch of road—to be passed on to immigrant families.

After Dmitri was sent to the principal's office the rest of us went off and, kinetically charged from the alter-cation, we played our football game. And while it would be impossible to attribute it to that frigid day, I fell ill with a cold that had me bedridden for the next four days—the same four days Dmitri was suspended. When we both returned the following week, I walked up to Dmitri as he was opening his locker.

"I couldn't talk to Steph like that," I said.

Dmitri stared at me. He had a button nose, thin at its bridge and round at the end, and pale blue eyes that contrasted sharply with his black hair. His hair wasn't long and wasn't short, and in the front it was trimmed into a line of inconsistent bangs.

Dmitri also had a thin moustache on his upper lip that appeared to be comprised of the first hair that had ever grown from those follicles. It was as if the ends of those hairs had been present when he was born; there was something ideological in his not shaving them, as if he was saying: "These hairs on my upper lip have picked up the smells and collected the invisible matter and seen everything there was to see from the first fifteen years of my existence, from the inside of my mother's womb to Moscow to Baltimore."

"What'd you say to get him so pissed?" I said.

"I asked him if we should wear gloves for cold," Dmitri said. "Then he asked me what. I told him if he wanted me to, I'd go get us some hand jobs."

I laughed, though Dmitri only cracked a smile. Then, from his locker, he pulled out a pair of stonewashed jeans and a black sweatshirt with the Baltimore Orioles logo on front. The plastic print was cracked, and there was a faint patch of gray on the right shoulder where it had come into contact with bleach at some point in its long life.

The sweatshirt had been mine. My mother had sent it to a synagogue rummage sale. It was so pilly from countless washings that for years I'd only worn it to bed. Before I left for Israel the previous summer my mother had sewn tiny cloth tags with my name into the collars of all my shirts. It had been the cause of a vicious argument between us before I left. Now Dmitri was walking around with that tag inside his shirt. I turned and walked away without saying anything else.

From then on, if I saw Dmitri in the hallway, I would pretend to open a locker and watch him. Mostly he and his friends stood up against the gunmetal lockers looking at their feet, aloof. I overheard his friends call him "Dmitri Abramovitch," which wasn't the last name Stephanopoulos called him in class. The only times Dmitri was away from this group he was with the most beautiful girl I had ever seen. Yelizaveta had pumice-black hair and pale white skin, soft and smooth unlike Dmitri's, which was pasty, and he was always composed around her. Like Dmitri, Yelizaveta had only started at Pikesville at the beginning of the previous year. I watched as they kissed on the cheek hello. It seemed there was nothing he could say that wouldn't make her laugh. When she laughed, the chirping sound rang like a clever song.

\*

A few weeks after I started paying Dmitri attention, fall assumed the quiddity of winter. Somehow we still were forced to march outside for gym class each afternoon. Dmitri stepped into his role as scapegoat in our gym class, and I became a restored teacher's pet. Dmitri now did duty fetching lacrosse goals from the equipment closet and collecting sodden towels at the end of class. Stephanopoulos forced him to run laps at the most innocuous offense, while I moved throughout the early winter weeks with utter impunity.

The last week of November brought one final limpid day. There were record highs into the sixties, and it had been an unseasonably dry month. There was dew instead of frost on the grass and the sun came out early, straining a pale yellow through the diffuse scrim of fog. That day, Steph volunteered me to help Dmitri bring out the bag of rubber-laced, imitation-leather footballs.

"Zilber," Stephanopoulos said. "Take Gerson with you and grab the flags and balls from the closet."

"I will not!" Dmitri said.

He said it too loudly, but his face evinced no embarrassment. The whole class hushed.

"I will do it myself," Dmitri said.

Dmitri had caught me looking at him a few times during those past few weeks. Feeling like some strange interloper, I'd always averted my eyes when he saw me. Maybe Dmitri had grown weary of me. While he was gracious enough to keep up a bit of camaraderie, he wasn't without his pride. Stephanopoulos viewed his refusal as undistilled truculence.

"Look who's turned into a real man!" he said. "Why don't you drop your pants and show us who's a man?"

Dmitri smoldered. Again he said, "I will not."

"Now Gerson," Stephanopoulos said, "get over to the damn closet and get a hand on those balls." A snicker rippled through the group. "Dmitri, go with Gerson and the rest of us will see you out on the playing field. Dmitri, two laps when you're done. Gerson, you're running with him."

The boys' locker room was down a short flight of stairs from the rest of the high school. It reeked the cloying reek of teenage sweat. Dmitri walked through it, picked up two huge bags of footballs. He was headed back into the room to grab the flags we would wear to delineate our teams. But then he walked back to me, put a hand on my shoulder, and turned to me so we were face to face.

"I have taken care of it," he said. "You go and grab bags and we take them out."

We walked out to the girls' softball fields, which were confined by a chain-linked fence and circumscribed by a red clay track. Dmitri dropped his bag of footballs. There were hundreds of girls playing on the fields.

"We go down now," Dmitri said. He gave me a look I recognized—an expression of a son looking at his father as he awaits some inarguable line of reasoning he'd be forced to follow. I could have decided against following Dmitri. I had the choice to steer him from trouble.

"We'd better put these bags somewhere in case someone comes," I said. In the short period we had known each other, Dmitri had rarely smiled, but he did now.

"Bring it here," he said. We stashed the bags in the trees next to the football field and stopped at the fence at the bottom of the hill. Dmitri grabbed one of the metal links and let his weight fall back, his chin down against the tops of his hands. In the middle of the track there were two hundred high school girls, all dressed in identical gym uniforms—purple shirts clinging to their bodies, gray nylon shorts swaying off their young hips. The uniforms stole something of their physical disctinctions, leaving them defined instead by their competitive personas, their gaits and speed.

Dmitri walked along the fence, and he called out to Yelizaveta. She stopped and turned. Yelizaveta was five-feet-seven, and her straight black hair fell to the middle of her shoulder blades, tied up at the base of her head with green elastic. She looked at Dmitri and shook her head. She said something that sounded firm but loving. Then she turned to me.

My hands felt like something I'd stolen. My gym shorts had no pockets. I folded my arms across my chest, hands up under my armpits. Yelizaveta cocked her head with no small intimation of coquettishness.

"Hello," she said. She turned to Dmitri. "Who is it you brings?"

Dmitri looked at me as if he was as embarrassed by my hands as I was.

"Samuel from gym class," he said.

"Liza," the squat gym teacher called. "Liza, what have I told you about talking to boys in class?" Then she looked at Dmitri and me. Keeping her gaze locked on him she said, "And just what do you two think you're doing here?"

Yelizaveta called back at her, "Ms. Leonard, is my brother. He tells me something about mother. How I will be going home to school end of day." She turned her eyes to Ms. Leonard with the same sultry confidence she had directed at me just a moment earlier.

"All right then," Ms. Leonard said. "But let's get back on to class, then."

Concentrated afternoon sunlight beamed down on granite rocks as we walked back up the hill. The sounds of girls at their games carried up to us in dithyrambs amid my reverie. We came to the rock where we had stashed the footballs.

"That was quick thinking, Yelizaveta saying you were her brother," I said.

Dmitri knitted his brow.

"Yelizaveta is my sister," he said. "Is not some idea— is just truth. I always tell only truth."

"Oh," I said. "I just had always assumed that she was your girlfriend. I just always thought."

"Yes. It has been impossible not to see you are looking at her. Yelizaveta always thinks everyone is looking at her. Same when you walk by us in hallways. She wants everyone to look at her. She is like me in some ways."

"How do you mean?" I said.

"I am—well, it is what I am," Dmitri said. He paused. He put his hands on his hips. He pushed his shoulder blades closer together like a catapult drawn back to fire. "I am a sensualist," he said. "Do you know what sensualist is? Like in novels of Dostoyevsky." I shook my head. The word made me think of scented massage oils, hairy-chested men from the '70s. We had been assigned *Crime and Punishment* in sophomore English but I hadn't read it. The cover seemed too dark, the figure on it too bearded.

"Like in Dostoyevsky!" Dmitri said, as if by saying it louder he might make me admit to having read it. "Like Prince Myshkin or Dmitri Karamazov. I don't care what people think of me. I say what I feel, when I feel it, and do what I like when I like. Also, Dmitri Karamazov is who my father names me after. Sometimes my mother calls me 'Mitya,' though I do not like it if she does it. Is better she calls me Dmitri."

"I don't like it when my father calls me Sammy," I said.

"If you like, as we are friends," Dmitri said, "you can call me by my name with patronymic. Dmitri Abramovitch. Is show of friendship." Then Stephanopoulos' voice hit us like we'd been jolted from a book we were reading together.

"What kind of bullshit horseplay is this!" he said. He was only ten paces from us. "How hard can it be to get a couple of bags of balls?"

"Some of footballs spilled from bag. It has hole in it," Dmitri said.

"Don't bullshit me, boy," Steph said.

"I am not bullshit," Dmitri said. "We are sweating. Have we not been running? We do not want balls spilled all around ground."

"He's not lying," I said. I reached down and flipped the bag over. Though none of the balls came out, the hole was substantial.

"All right, get those bags up and let's get over there and play some football. But first I want three laps." We picked the balls up and headed toward the field while Stephanopoulos stood. "And Zilber, I'm watching you," Steph said. "You slip up, son, I'll be there to put you down."

Dmitri took off ahead of me. He was fast at first, but by the middle of our second lap he slowed, and I caught him inside the first turn. His face was pale. Too many cigarettes to run that much. I felt it too. We both walked for a minute. Steph yelled, "Pick it up! You're not walking those laps. Hup to!"

When we started again I slowed my pace to match Dmitri's. He affected a runner's gait. We ran next to each other. Though I could have run much faster, now we didn't hear from Steph again. I moved my arms as if I was exerting a great force of energy, and Dmitri did the same.

We ran together that way until we were done.

# TWO

Dmitri first came to sit in my car on a Tuesday, first week in December. Each morning since I'd inherited my parents' weather-worn decade-old beige 1979 Volvo DL station wagon the year before—they had two, the other an '83—I arrived at school and pulled into my regular parking spot. The other kids would sit together in their factory-new Ford Probes and Camaros and Mustangs, the bass turned all the way up in their custom speakers. The mornings had grown cold, so I would roll my window down just low enough for the smoke of my cigarette to sneak out, just low enough that someone might hear music coming from my radio and come sit with me. It hadn't happened until that morning Dmitri Zilber walked up. He knocked on my window.

"Let me have cigarette," Dmitri said. He got in and I handed him one and he lit it. "Is good cigarette," Dmitri said. "I smoke USA Gold. Thicker. Or for really good, Marlboro Red. But this is good."

"It's a Camel," I said. "Camel Filter."

"Camel Filter," Dmitri said. "Best good ones I've had are Marlboro Red. But I like Camel Filter now." He dragged on the cigarette. "I have thought about it," he said. "When you like to call me Dmitri Abramovitch, would be OK."

"Sure," I said. "Sure, I'll do that." Dmitri gave a curt nod, shrugged and looked at me with the corners of his mouth just barely upturned. He got out of the car and took off.

Later that night I met up with Tanya Weiss at Weiss's Deli, her parents' restaurant, out on Reisterstown Road. She was already sitting at our table.

"I heard you were smoking with some Russian kid in your car this morning," Tanya said. She was picking at the doughy insides of a scooped-out bagel. My face flushed.

"I bummed this guy from gym class a cigarette," I said.

"I've been meaning to talk to you about your smoking, young man," Tanya said.

"It's not like you smoke with me in my car."

"You know I volunteer at the office in the mornings. These are the kinds of things that will get a young woman into a top-tier university. It wouldn't hurt her best friend to try and bolster his transcript in some corresponding manner."

"So we're on to the mid-century in this book," I said.

Tanya frowned. She pulled out her history book. We went over some World War II stuff we were studying. Soon we were deep into the last couple chapters of the textbook, moving briskly through our reading, in routine. "So the Americans were pulled into the war in 1944, but not before providing the British with the warships that Churchill had requested in 1942, long before the Lend-Lease Act—"

"Look," Tanya said. "You've got some new friend I don't know. When was the last time you had a new friend? I know all the people you know, Samuel Gerson. I'm curious." Tanya's father had just come out of his office behind the deli counter. He was a short balding little homunculus, a former University of Maryland tennis player who worked in shorts to show off his oversized calves.

"What say, Sam?" he said.

"Uh, just a little studying, Mr. Weiss," I said. "Thanks for the fries."

"You think the Moose will develop that knuckle curve in the off-season like the O's say he will?"

"Guess he'd better."

"And what about your arm, son? From what I was hearing, you're a curveball away from being our number two starter."

"Can't say I've been working much."

"Better get to work," Mr. Weiss said. "Make us proud."

"Look, we're trying to study here, Dad," Tanya said.

"Ok, Ok," Mr. Weiss said before he took off.

The story of Tanya's family was better known than any family in Pikesville. Weiss's was the longest-running deli on Reisterstown Road, the center of all the kibitzing in the community since before the Jews of Pikesville even were the Jews of Pikesville. When Tanya's father was our age his parents owned the original Weiss's on Lombard Street, on a block in East Baltimore known as Corned Beef Row. One night while Tanya's grandparents were closing, Tanya's grandmother counting out the day's receipts, two men walked into the restaurant wearing masks, pulled out guns and demanded the money from the register. And Chaim Weissheim, who had been on the beach at Omaha and had been awarded a Bronze Medal and three Purple Hearts—Chaim Wessheim, who was a community leader by temperment and by sheer accident of chronology—tried to stop the robbery.

The gunmen shot him twice in the head, then his wife.

Tanya's father was sent to live with his aunt and uncle. It would take twenty years for Tanya's great-uncle and then her father to get the Weissheims' delis back on track. By then the whole family had settled into Pikesville, and while Tanya grew up without a grandfather, she grew up with the legacy of his heroism, and a father whose hagiography was written every time that story was passed like samizdat between Pikesville's Jews.

While Tanya went over our history homework, I went to get a sandwich. When I came back she'd already finished her work.

"I hear that kid you smoked with in your car has a hot sister," Tanya said.

"Do you," I said. Tanya jabbed her finger in the middle of my Reuben. She pulled out a piece of corned beef.

"I don't understand how you can eat this greasy shit," Tanya said. "I know you're not playing baseball anymore, but you could still stand to take care of yourself. You don't want to turn into a fatty."

"The proceeds from that greasy shit will pay for your college education."

"Grease gives you acne," Tanya said. She swiped her greasy finger across my nose. "Don't think you'll be free of acne for long now." She lifted her history book and pointed to a page far before the chapter we were meant to be studying. "Ok, let's get back to this. We were looking at Operation Overlord, right?" Tanya said. "You really ought to study this stuff so you'll do well and go to a good college. Because if you don't go to a good college, how will you ever escape this shtetl?"

"Ok, Ok," I said. "I never said I was going to do anything of the sort."

"Never said you wanted to leave this town, Gerson?" Tanya said. "Is that not all you've wanted since the day I met you? For you it's like some kind of injury every time you have to talk to anyone but me. And now this kid you're smoking with."

Tanya picked up the top piece of bread from my sandwich and put the corned beef she'd taken back on the stack of meat. "Eat up, boubby," she said. "This food doesn't grow on trees, you know."

I drove Tanya home. The Weissheims were the Weisses now, and they lived in a gated community down Reisterstown Road, in Owings Mills. Theirs was a large five-bedroom colonial. It was mostly red brick and white shutters. I'm not sure it was that much bigger than my parents' house, but the Weiss' subdivision, built only a couple of years before, was the most desirable in our whole area. The houses on either side of it and across the street looked identical. There were two large flowerbeds out front. A scattering of mulch had been dusted out onto the cobblestone walkway leading to the front door.

"Well, I don't mean to make you feel caged in talking about this Dmitri. But if I don't look out for you, Samuel Gerson, who will? Now give me a kiss on the cheek and let us part with this understanding."

She got out of the car and walked to her door. On the way she kicked at the displaced mulch in the walkway with her white Stan Smiths, then bent down to wipe away any mulch particles from their pristine toes. Tanya Weiss's feet would never stay dirty long.

*

A couple weeks passed after Dmitri smoked that cigarette in my car before I approached him outside of gym class. It was just before Christmas break, and with the anticipation of freedom, the high school parking lot was littered with groups of students standing, shivering and smoking cigarettes. I was talking with a couple of my old baseball teammates when, not twenty feet from where I was standing, Dmitri's friends walked away from him and left him standing alone. He had on my old Orioles sweatshirt.

"Hey, Dmitri," I said. "How's it going?" He pushed up off of the back of the Honda he was leaning on. He looked at me, his face not betraying any emotion.

"No, no. Not now," he said. "Can't you see I'm busy?" I turned to see that Dmitri's friends were standing in front of Jeremy Goldstein. He was the tailback for the football team and the catcher on the baseball team— my old battery mate—and a big kid, six-foot-two, two-hundred pounds. I'd known Goldstein since we first played little league together in the first grade. His father was a surgeon at Johns Hopkins, like his father before him, and his father before. They were Viennese

Jews who had come over in the antebellum period,
settled into Baltimore so long before the war that the
bellum during the time of their emigration was ante
the war between states not European, but American.
A Goldstein had worked as a battlefield medic for the
Union Army in Virginia, had served at Appomattox,
and the Goldsteins had claimed him as their forebearer,
though who knows if this was true. Those who have
been around enough generations have the luxury of
telling unverifiable stories as if they were fact.

Now the scion of this family who had for so long
tended to the wounded in the US was surrounded by
Dmitri's friends. Serge Volynskiy and Alex Ferdyshchenko
stood in front of Goldstein, with Fy Warchawski right
behind them. Benny Dudkin was to his side. Two of
Jeremy's friends from the football team stood next to him.

The group erupted in a chaos of punches and kicks,
panting and wrestling. Serge and Alex attacked Goldstein
while the others formed a semi-circle around him to
fend off his friends. Not many of the punches landed
on Goldstein's head, though they were compact and
expert. Benny, even for his massive head of curls, looked
like a middle-weight boxer. Alex got a couple of good
punches in when Goldstein was tied up with Benny.
I'd seen plenty of lunchroom brawls and most were just
like this—a few punches glancing off their intended

targets, a lot of pushing, holding, grasping at clothing to catch one's breath.

The fighters were all reduced to a grappling, exhausted mass with Goldstein at the bottom. Serge had taken over the role of lookout once the fight was underway and when he saw a pair of teachers leaving the building, he yelled and pulled away the two attacking Goldstein. Goldstein rose from the middle of the scuffle, the tumescent redness around his eyes of a boxer between late rounds. A trickle of blood dripped from his nose.

"I'll kill you," he said. He yelled in their direction like he wasn't entirely sure he meant it, like it was just what you say in that situation. He was dazed and breathless. The two baseball players shuffled him off into his car and drove away. The approaching teachers pulled Serge and Fy into the school.

All during the fight Dmitri stood, his feet planted on the macadam. When the first punches were thrown he had taken a couple of steps in the direction of the action but then stayed. His eyes squinted and showed some opaque reaction. His hands were now tight, clasping and unclasping fists. Benny and Alex came over and got into Benny's car, a ten-year-old Honda Accord covered in patches of scabrous rust. As soon as the teachers walked off with their friends, the three Russians drove away.

By the next afternoon we'd all heard that because he went to Owings Mills, Fy had been passed over to the principal there. Our principal, Mr. Broz, expelled Serge the next day. He'd been on probation already, and this was one fight too many. He was sent to Hickey. Mr. Broz knew that Goldstein and his two teammates were the combatants on the other side of the fight. He called them into the office the next day, too. They told their side of the story—they'd been attacked by the Russians and were defending themselves—and they marched in their friends to tell the same story. Though there was a strict suspension policy at the school for fights, Mr. Broz let them off with a warning.

\*

After dinner that night I pulled out the phone book. I thumbed through it for some time.

"What you looking for?" my mother said. She walked over to the cabinet and then dropped a slimmer book in front of me. "Better luck with the White Pages."

She left the room. Somehow she knew just what I was looking for without my even asking for it. Zilber was right there, under the Z's. A woman's voice came on the line.

"Hallo," she said.

"Uh, hi. Is Dmitri there?"

"Who is it?"

"Uh…it's a friend of his. From school."

"This does not sounds like Dmitri's friend."

"No, not one of his Russian…not one of his regular friends. This is Samuel. Sam. Gerson."

"Dmitri does not knows who is Samuel Gerson."

"From gym class. Samuel from gym class."

"Oh."

There was a lot of commotion in the background on her end, like she was standing beside a construction site. Then it stopped.

"Samuel in gym class," she said. There was an interminable silence on the line.

"So is Dmitri home?"

"Samuel, you come visit Dmitri at home sometimes."

"How do you mean?"

"I mean just what it is."

There was a longer silence, followed by a click on the line. The phone sounded airier.

"Mom, I'm on the phone," I said.

"Yes. He looks for Dmitri."

"Oh, sorry," my mother said. "Who is this? Tanya? That doesn't sound like Tanya."

"Who is?" Yelizaveta said.

"Mom," I said.

"This is Samuel's mother," my mother said. "Why don't you introduce yourself, honey."

"Mom?" I said, louder.

"No. Not Tanya. Yelizaveta Zilber. I tells Samuel that he comes. Visits Dmitri."

"Mom," I said.

"Tonight is a school night," my mother said. "But I'm sure Samuel would like to come over when it's not a school night."

"Please hang up the phone," I said.

It was silent again on the line.

"So is Dmitri home or not?" I said.

"No. Who is Tanya?"

"Tanya is no one."

"This I would not like you to say about me."

"Well."

"Maybe you come."

"Will you please tell Dmitri I called?"

"I'm sure he will be happy you calls. What is your numbers?"

I gave her the number.

"Well, thanks."

"Welcome. 133 Greenhill. You need to know if you come."

We hung up. My mother had come back into the kitchen. She stood and washed the dishes.

"Who's this Dmitri?" my mother said.

"He's no one," I said. "He's a friend."

"Well we've never met him before," my mother said.

"Why don't you invite him over for dinner sometime? We're having salmon one day later this week."

"He's not that kind of friend," I said.

"How would you know if you don't ask? Sounds like you're assuming a lot about this friend without asking."

"Oᴋ," I lied. "I'll ask."

Upstairs in my room there was only static on the television so I put on a ᴄᴅ as loud as I could. I sat down to read. Then I put down the book. I called Tanya.

"So you saw that whole fight," she said.

"It was kind of boring."

"Nothing worse than boring violence," Tanya said. "But your new friend was involved, huh? You should be careful with that kid."

"He didn't do anything," I said. "He just stood there. Weird. What do you think those kids have against Goldstein?"

Tanya said she hadn't heard anything. I said she should try to find out.

We hung up.

I tried to read, but it was no use, so I went to my window, packed a bowl, and cracked the window. Outside a robin picked at a plastic bag stuck up in a tree. What was a robin doing out this late in the season? And at night? It jerked its head in my direction. It had a questioning look on its face—its head clicked in one

direction, and then, barely perceptibly, in another.
It moved its head so fast you couldn't see how it had
gotten from one position to the next. The yard was
mostly black. We were close enough to the city that the
sky glowed pink like the insulation you find in spools
in attics—not bright, but light enough I could see the
lawn, where a fox skittered across the yard chasing after
something. I put my bowl down and tried to focus, but
the fox had moved out of range. Not long after the bowl
was cashed it skittered back across with something hanging from its mouth, something small and squirming in
the candy-pink light.

# THREE

Tanya wouldn't have time to find out what animosity pre-existed between Dmitri and Goldstein before I experienced it firsthand. Wednesday afternoon the next week I was leaving school a period early. There'd been a substitute in history, and it provided an easy chance to sneak out one of the school's many side doors rarely monitored by the security guards who policed the school, looking for truants. Outside the door, I saw Dmitri stalking away from campus. He was alone. I picked up my pace. Just as I was about to call Dmitri's name, Jeremy Goldstein and Steinbart came around the corner. Goldstein was goofing around as he always was, arms gesticulating wildly from his sides.

As they walked up, Goldstein's face blanched, then hardened into a scowl. Steinbart nodded his head in Dmitri's direction. Goldstein jerked up straight. Then his body went slack. He looked at Steinbart, who looked back at him as if asking a question.

Then Goldstein fell into an affected swagger. Dmitri squared his shoulders. He stopped. Again, just as they had when his friends fought Goldstein in the parking lot, his hands balled up into tight fists.

"What's up," Goldstein said.

Dmitri said nothing. Goldstein stepped closer to him.

"Where'd you get those cool gold chains? Steal them somewhere?"

Goldstein put his fingers on the chains and let them drop on Dmitri's chest. Dmitri stood his ground. He said:

"I do not steal. I get your mother to buy them for me when I see her this weekend."

Goldstein was thrown off. He hardly reacted at all to the comment. Then he said:

"Fuck you. You're nothing without your little friends around. Why don't you try some shit now, instead of getting your Russians to do it for you?"

Still none of the three of them saw me standing by the side of the school. Dmitri took a couple of steps back.

"What, you can't stick up for yourself without your Communist friends?" Goldstein said. "Or maybe we'd have something to talk about if your hot sister was around and I could tell her what's what, just like last time?"

Dmitri flew at him. He did not lose control. Instead he bent down, running and crouching, picked up a handful of dirt and threw it in Goldstein's eyes, his left knee crossing his right and his right arm crossing his chest like a shortstop gunning for first. Goldstein's hands went up to his face. He was spitting out dirt when Dmitri slammed into him with his shoulder. He got right up inside Goldstein like a boxer and swung two quick uppercuts at Goldstein's chin.

The second punch mashed Goldstein's lip against his teeth. He spit again, and some blood came from his mouth. Dmitri punched him twice more in the stomach. Then Dmitri balled the fabric of Goldstein's T-shirt up in his fists and tried to throw him to the ground. Goldstein must have outweighed Dmitri by at least thirty pounds—but he was enraged. He windmilled his hands around at the crown of Dmitri's head, landing four or five glancing punches as the two of them fell to the ground together.

I'd never seen as brazen a first move as Dmitri had just pulled, and from the stunned look on Steinbart's face, neither had he. But now he saw the blood that stained the collar of Goldstein's T-shirt, and he rushed at them. It looked as if he might try to pry Dmitri off his teammate. Instead he threw punches at Dmitri's sides. When he saw that he couldn't get a solid shot that way—the two of them were rolling around too much—he pulled not at Dmitri but at Goldstein, so that they were both on top of Dmitri. Steinbart dug his knee into Dmitri's shoulder. Goldstein held down the other shoulder with his hand, which was now shaking.

Dmitri was pinned. Jeremy Goldstein grabbed my new friend's shirt in his fist. He pushed up under Dmitri's neck at his jaw line, shoving his head back against the ground. He landed two heavy punches on Dmitri's chin. A hiss escaped Goldstein's mouth as blood from his lip smeared across Dmitri's face. The punches landed hard on Dmitri's head, and some of Dmitri's spirit fell from him with the trauma.

Act, don't act.

In the past, I'd never have gotten near a fight.

Never.

My first punch hit Goldstein's shoulder. I got two more punches in, both on his head. I plowed into him with my shoulder. It felt great. If Goldstein was thirty pounds bigger than Dmitri, he was forty pounds heavier than me. He fell back to his left knee. He did not lose his balance. Goldstein spun toward me, and in the process he threw a sharp elbow to my jaw. He sloughed me off like I was a yapping hound. I landed hard on a rock behind me, and a dashing pain went through my forearm. My whole body felt instantly desiccated, the middle of my chest hollowed out and arid. I'd just started to get up off the ground, rolled ten feet away from them, when I heard a man's voice saying, "Hey! Hey! You sallies better stop with your dancing!"

Steph.

*

"I haven't ever seen you in here before, Gerson, have I?" Mr. Broz said. He'd just suspended Dmitri. Now it was my turn. He sat behind his low desk, which was covered in wood-grain laminate. He was a corpulent middle-aged man, five-foot-eight, with a thinning shock of gray Slavic hair and round, ruddy cheeks like bruised peaches. Every day Mr. Broz wore the same mustard-yellow houndstooth jacket and blue wool pants. He wore a blue-and-white striped Oxford tie, knotted high and wide under his substantial jowls, and he spoke with a light Baltimore drawl—water was "wooder," wash "worsch." When we read "Bartleby" in my sophomore English class, I pictured Mr. Broz.

There was a photograph of Ronald Reagan in a cowboy hat and cowboy boots on the wall over Mr. Broz's right shoulder. Over his left shoulder there was a photograph of Eisenhower—not President Eisenhower, but General Eisenhower, Supreme Allied Commander, all uniform, medals, stars, epaulettes and that cold white baggy-eyed stare, a look Mr. Broz seemed to be attempting to emulate. On the wall to his right hung an 8x10 photo of Newt Gingrich, signed and personalized.

As Mr. Broz looked at me I rubbed the bruise on the side of my head, which was now rapidly knotting on my skull. The sharp pain in my arm throbbed with the quickening beat of my heart.

"What kind of student are you, Gerson?" he said.

"What do you mean?"

"I mean exactly what I asked," he said. His nostrils flared but his eyes were fixed on me. Those eyes said he was composed now, but if I wanted things to work out, I had better be willing to have the conversation he wanted.

"Well, I get good grades, if that's what you mean."

"An A student—that's what you are," he said. "You're an A student. Don't you take pride in that fact, son? Don't you know what kinds of opportunity the world has to offer a young man who walks the line?"

"I didn't do anything but try to help—"

Mr. Broz just held up his hand. The air in the room was close. It smelled antiseptic, a bathroom just scoured with bleach. My arm throbbed.

"You don't understand it now, what you can make of yourself, Samuel Gerson. You probably think what we do here has no purpose. That we punish or have rules just to be mean, that we don't listen to reason but only dole out suspensions, expulsions. Don't you." I expected him to stop there, but Mr. Broz was far from finished with me. "Don't you, Mr. Gerson?"

"I guess there's a certain draconian aspect to what you guys do here."

"A certain—right. Very smart. SAT vocabulary, Mr. Gerson, the kind that can take you far. Right. This isn't a democracy. You're not free here. What would you say, Mr. Gerson, is the most draconian thing we do?"

"I'm not sure I know what you mean," I said.

"Just what I said. What thing do we do to you that feels the most egregious to you? I assume you know that one, Mr. Gerson. Egregious."

"Sure," I said. "Well. Um. Ok, then I guess I'd have to say hall passes."

"Right!" Mr. Broz said. It was like a small bark, loud enough that I jumped a little in my seat, which made him wince, like he hadn't meant to speak quite so loudly. "That's exactly right. Just what I was fishing for. You hate hall passes. Seems completely extraneous you should have to carry a pass to get out of a room to use the bathroom. At home you don't have to use a hall pass—your left-leaning parents would let you do just about anything you chose. So why shouldn't the same happen here? But, Mr. Gerson, that's not how things will be when you reach the real world. We're here to prepare you for that."

Mr. Broz stopped. He looked up at the ceiling. He rolled his head around and there was a loud popping in the back of his neck. There were a thousand little red bumps of razor burn under his chin.

"You go to the airport much?" Mr. Broz said. I shook my head. "Do you know what happens in the airport,

Mr. Gerson? What does one do in the airport?" Eat at McDonald's, I thought. Avoid having to use the bathrooms. "Do you know when you walk by and there are those rooms and all those rooms say 'VIP Club' on them? They're all over the airport. Do you know them?"

I nodded.

"Haven't you seen that there is always a place to swipe a card? See, Mr. Gerson, if you don't belong in the VIP room—if you are not a Very Special Person and so people don't want you to come into their room for Very Special People—you cannot get in. It's no different from what you get here at school. You're here to be prepared to act as you're meant to act in the real world. Right? It's no different with your behavior! You've almost joined the adult world now, Mr. Gerson. Young man. They call you young man because that's what you are. The kinds of people you associate with here in high school, the kinds of friendships you make—they might last. Possibly you'll speak to these people again when you're my age. More likely, you won't."

Again he stopped.

"Do you know how many of my friends from high school I still talk to, Mr. Gerson? None. Not one. I haven't seen or heard from a single one of them in more than twenty years. But do you know what will really matter? What matters is who the other people remember you as. What matters is who the other people remember you were friends with. I know people, Samuel, who went to law school. To Harvard Law School. And while they were there they strutted around thinking they were smart. In mock negotiations they wouldn't be afraid to step on toes. They felt because they were smart it didn't matter who was their friends. Well, when they became lawyers, they had to practice against those same people. In a courtroom, Mr. Gerson, they had to see those people."

Mr. Broz stopped for what must have been thirty seconds. Just when it occurred to me that perhaps he was expecting me to say something, he started again.

"Look, Mr. Gerson," Mr. Broz said. "I suspended those other boys for a week. Goldstein and Steinbart are going to miss their next-to-last football game. And Dmitri Zilber. Dmitri was suspended. I'm going light, and I'm giving you two weeks detention. I don't expect to see you in here again. I suspect that you'll find you're going to be more careful with the kinds of relationships you maintain in the future."

He put out his hand. I'd never shaken hands with a teacher before. My wrist hurt so I could barely stand it. Between the sweat of my palm and the sweat of his it was as if we'd never even touched.

*

The next day the pain in my wrist got too bad for me to handle. My mother took me to the doctor. I had a hairline fracture. I got a cast—not one of those old plaster things, but a transparent, removable plastic shell. It changed my appearance in a subtle yet undeniable way. I was marked, adorned, equipped. On the ride home from the doctor, my mother couldn't hold her tongue any longer.

"Samuel," she said. "Did you really break that arm playing football?"

"Yeah," I said.

"Something just seems off about it."

I reached forward to turn the temperature down. "Isn't this a little early in the season for heat?" I said.

"I was cold." She reached forward to turn the heat down even further. Some droplets of water had come to cover my window with condensation. I watched as one made its jerky way down with the vagaries of the wind outside.

"I got detention for two weeks," I said.

"For playing football?" my mother said.

"No," I said. "For fighting."

My mother hit the brakes and the car kicked. Then she put her foot on the gas pedal and we sailed forward again.

"Samuel Isaac. With who?"

"Jeremy Goldstein," I said. "I saw him beating up my friend Dmitri. I couldn't just stand by and watch, you know? I couldn't just stand by and watch."

A new glare illuminated the numinous windshield. Some lucid gossamer had built up above the vents in front of me. I reached forward with my broken arm and whisked them away.

She reached and rolled down her window. "Maybe you're right," she said. "It's a sunny day."

It was too cold to keep it down for long—it got to be freezing in the car inside of two minutes—but she didn't reach to roll it up.

"You played baseball with Jeremy," my mother said. "Your father knows Isaac from work."

"He's kind of an asshole."

"And you've got a broken arm, Samuel."

"It appears that way."

She looked at me sharply, ready to chastise me for my impertinence, but then her expression shifted. "Who is this Dmitri boy?"

"A friend," I said.

Gelid air was blowing in through my mother's window. I could tell she was just as cold as I was, but she didn't move to change it. She looked at me, waiting for me to continue. I reached to put the heat back on.

*

Sunday afternoon I drove to the Zilbers' for the first time. Greenhill was a huge neighborhood of subsidized housing a couple of miles from my house. We all used to go there every October for Halloween—it was the neighborhood with the most houses in one concentrated area. 133 Greenhill Avenue was at the bottom of a long hill, houses toward the bottom perched on the city border. Most of the Russian Jews who came to Pikesville were set up with apartments there. Yelizaveta came to the door.

"Oh," she said. "You here for me, or is for Dmitri?"

"Is this an Oᴋ time?" I said.

"Always is Oᴋ time," Yelizaveta said. She led me into the kitchen, where a woman in tight stone-washed jeans and a baggy Champion sweatshirt sat at the kitchen table. Even in her house clothes Mrs. Zilber was elegant. She had a smooth young face and long eyelashes. Her eyes had a feline narrowness intensified by the fact that in sweats in her own kitchen she wore heavy indigo eyeliner. Mrs. Zilber's hair was straight and flat to her head, pulled back tight with a green-and-gold sparkled rubber band. She looked remarkably like Yelizaveta.

"Mama," Yelizaveta said. Her mother didn't look up. "Mama," Yelizaveta said again, this time shoving her mother in the shoulder. Her flirtatious affect was gone, as if she'd momentarily forgotten I was there. Mrs. Zilber looked up at me. She looked me up and down. Then her eyes fell back to the television.

"Da, Liza, Da," she said.

"This is mother," Yelizaveta said. "She is making cards to sell for business. Busy. We go down." There was no evidence of any work before Mrs. Zilber of any kind—she was watching TV.

Downstairs was a large unfinished basement. The walls were all gray concrete. In one corner was an old Apple IIe on a short table. It was covered with Baltimore Orioles stickers. In the other was a 27-inch television set with an Atari attached. Over against a wall was a pile of unopened Barbie Doll boxes in Glad bags, and in a basket next to them about fifty Beanie Babies. Stashed behind them I saw a weathered collection of '50s hardtop suitcases, the kind with chrome latches that you pushed open. Dmitri sat in a blue beanbag chair reading a book. There was a hole in the chair, and with any movement a steady stream of tiny white Styrofoam balls poured out from it.

"Hello, Samuel," Dmitri said. "I did not know you would come." He made no move to get up. Dmitri pointed to his book. "Do you know this novel?"

The book's title was written in Russian.

"I don't read it," I said.

"Many Americans don't read," Dmitri said. "But I did not expect it from you!" He hadn't understood that

I meant I couldn't read Russian. Before I had a chance
to correct him, Dmitri said, "Is too bad. You are smart.
I know when someone is smart. We always learn from
our father we must read. This is Dostoyevsky's *Idiot*.
Do I tell you of his books?

"Here Dostoyevsky tells of Prince Myshkin, who is
Dostoyevsky himself. Myshkin eventually has seizures,
is epilepsy, as Dostoyevsky himself had. But Myshkin
never does any exactly rational thing, and with him are
friends, especially small boy named Ippolit and wild,
violent man named Rogozhin, who crashes parties and
forces himself into houses where he is not wanted."

"What's so great about it?"

"What is so great? All is great! As with Dmitri Karamazov,
these men do as they feel when they feel, and they feel
all very much. They are sensualists. Today people hide
feelings—if they are angry, if they are depressed, they
want to talk to psychiatrist so they don't show feelings.
They get in fight in school, school send them to ther-
apist. But why shouldn't we feel all times? What man
would not want to act as he feel?"

I told him I guessed he must be right. Dmitiri watched
me as if he expected me to continue, so I said the first
thing that came to my mind: "Is your father here?"

Dmitri and Yelizaveta looked at each other.

"Is not come to Baltimore yet," Yelizaveta said.

"Oh," I said. "I'm sorry."

"You are guest," Dmitri said. "You are friend. You can ask what you like. Our father is not come yet. He will be."

Yelizaveta only stared at me.

"I'm really sorry," I said.

"Do not be sorry! This is what I say. You ask friend question about thing that matters to him and to you and then apologize. Not to apologize!"

"Right," I said.

For a long time we played video games. Dmitri was an expert at *Space Invaders*, and Yelizaveta slayed me at two-player *Frogger*. At one point the game froze; Yelizaveta fixed it by blowing into the game console, her face lit by the blue wash the television screen cast over her face. It was nearly dark out and the basement was black save for that glow. Between games Yelizaveta smoked.

"That's OK?" I said.

"Smoke if you like," Dmitri said.

"Your mother must know that you smoke," I said.

Yelizaveta nodded. "House is small." She twisted the filter of her cigarette between her fingers.

"Oh—I just meant that the smoke would go upstairs."

"Is small. Don't say lies," she said. Her face fell just as it had earlier, when she talked to her mother. "Your house is bigger."

"I can't smoke at home."

Yelizaveta stubbed her cigarette out and she went back upstairs. I smoked quickly. Dmitri was preoccupied with his game. When he heard I had to go, Dmitri turned off the television.

"Please, you stay for dinner," he said.

"I really need to get home," I said.

He went back to playing his video game. Upstairs Mrs. Zilber was stirring a huge pot of soup in the kitchen while watching the evening news. A familiar smell arose from the pot, tones of paprika and meat wafted from the kitchen and a flash of standing outside my grandparents' house on Long Island lit in my mind: sharp paprika, cool winter air, diffuse yellow light of evening, the blurring incantation of grandpa's Magyar tongue. But it was too late now to change my mind and stay. Mrs. Zilber was still staring at the little television when I left. Yelizaveta walked me out.

"Samuel, when you return your vacation we goes out," Yelizaveta said.

"Oh," I said. "Oh, OK. A movie or something?"

"You have dinner," she said. "When you gets back, then I will sees house. Dinner. House and dinner."

I said OK. OK, we would have dinner. We would.

# FOUR

Every year during Christmas vacation the Gersons went up to the cold gray of Wantagh, New York to visit my grandparents on Long Island. This would be our first time up there since my grandmother died the spring before. On Christmas Eve my parents packed up our 1983 mint green Volvo DL wagon. We rode up I-95 to Long Island to spend a week in my grandfather's grim Hungarian shtetl. All of our focus was on Grandpa—he was looking pasty and thin, not taking great care of himself with his wife of fifty years gone.

Grandpa didn't cook for us, but that paprika smell from the Zilbers' still overwhelmed my grandmother's old kitchen. The yellow light of winter evenings rose in the afternoons there, and I found myself hating the place less than in the past. I even spoke to my grandfather some in earnest, mostly just to ask after his life without my grandmother.

"Is Oк, Samuel, is Oк," he said. "I did survive labor camp in Ukraine, I did survive labor camp in north of Budapest, I will survive now." His eyes were all watery when he said it, and while his eyes had always been glaucoma-wet, it seemed now it was something more. But that was all he said, and I'd heard the obfuscating phrases he used to avoid talking about his war experiences enough times I blanched at them now, and his breath smelled of decay—my father said he wasn't cleaning his dentures. For the rest of our stay, I gave myself over to the deadening wash of college football. But still something was tugging at me. Even if I couldn't have articulated it right then, I knew there was some new interest I had in him, something Dmitri and Yelizaveta had done. I didn't know enough yet to act on it. I won't say I believe now it would have changed anything, but maybe if I'd known what was to come a few months later, I could at least have spent that time talking to my grandfather.

I didn't. We came home the following Sunday evening, and the Monday back from Christmas vacation I stayed at the library until dinnertime. Outside, the lambent remnants of sunset brushed over the rooftops across the street from the high school. Dark was gathering over Baltimore's western suburbs.

"Samuel Gerson, you waits," Yelizaveta said. She wasn't quite running toward me, but every fourth or fifth step she would push up a bit on one leg or the other. "After break and you does not yet call. For dinner."

"I was going to. How's Dmitri?"

"Is fine," Yelizaveta said. Her eyes fell to my chest, across which lay my cast, held against me in a sling. She let her hand drift down onto it. She wasn't touching me; she was touching the hard plastic of the cast. But the weight of her arm against mine tightened the inside of my throat.

"It was fun playing *Frogger* the other day," I said, stupidly. Yelizaveta continued to look me directly in my eyes. A glint of light flashed off one of her dangling golden earrings. She placed her hand on the bare flesh of my upper arm.

"I am ready for us to have dinner one time," she said.

She smelled of cigarette smoke and sport deodorant. A car drove by and we both looked up. Its headlights passed across our faces. I put up my right hand to shade my eyes and hit myself in the forehead with my cast.

"You have plan for dinner?" she said.

"I just," I said. Then I said, "Come here."

I pulled her to me by her upper arms. I put my bare arm across the back of her neck and mashed the top of her head against my face. The move was clumsy, and after I had acted I hoped that at least some semblance of intimacy might come across. She pulled away. The momentary rejection of it made me want to grab her, hold her against me.

"I tell Dmitri you say hello," she said.

"Yeah, tell Dmitri that I say hello. That I will see him. Oĸ?"

I got in my car. In the rearview mirror I saw that Yelizaveta was watching. She had already lit another cigarette, and as I pulled away, the burning red ember glowing between Yelizaveta's fingers became the only thing clearly visible.

*

Yelizaveta was struggling in sophomore English, and in the days after holiday break she asked for my help. Although it was obvious enough within the first moments of an encounter with her that she needed it, Pikesville High School had failed to place Yelizaveta in an ESL class. Their reasoning was simple enough: they didn't have an ESL class. Still, Liza's English wasn't strong enough for her to negotiate the same terrain as the rest of her classmates, so she had asked me to help her with her paper on *The Great Gatsby*.

"We have to do this at your house," she said.

"Why?"

"We needs to do it on typewriter, and typewriter we has doesn't have ink."

My parents were going to be out on Thursday night, so I told her that I'd be happy to help, and asked if she wanted to come over at the end of the week.

As soon as Yelizaveta arrived we went out back and had a cigarette. I took her from the front door to the back step, though I knew she'd be taking in the particularities of my house just the same as I had hers months earlier. We smoked and then I invited her up to my room.

"So now you help me with homework," she said. She pushed me back and pulled the paper out from under me. I'd sat on it without realizing it was there. It had gotten all crinkled, so I smoothed out the wrinkles.

*There is this lady. Is called Daisy, who this man love— two man, really, and two man who love her*, the paper began. Soon it was covered in black ink. I pulled out the electronic typewriter my grandfather had bought me for my Bar Mitzvah and began typing the paper over. Each time I would find that the sentences I was writing were too lucid, their syntax too sophisticated, I went back and looked at Yelizaveta's original draft and muddied it to match hers. I was learning her language, learning to speak in her voice, and the more I read her sentences, the more I came to see that she had an advanced understanding of the novel.

"Hey," I said. "What did you think of Gatsby?"

"This man has love with woman, with Daisy," Yelizaveta said. "And he love her. But he try too hard too long, so when he have her, it get all…how you say? Well, is not good, I think. He can't have what he want."

"Well, he's willing to change his whole identity, his name and get rich all just so he can be with her."

"Is bad with her, too," Yelizaveta said. "With husband and all this."

"Ok—I think that part's clear in the paper. But you should acknowledge the other side of your argument. I mean, Daisy's not purely good."

"How is it?"

"Well, like this. She says right at the beginning, about her daughter, 'I hope she'll be a fool—that's the best thing a girl can be in this world, a beautiful little fool.'"

Yelizaveta scrunched her nose up. "She does not mean it."

"It's a superficial thing to say."

"She is with, uh, from house with rich and with husband who is bad," Yelizaveta said. "He is racism. He have another woman. So what Daisy say is bad. But she mean this thing about she is fool, and is, is, um, is sad. Is, uh, is. Depressed…yeah?"

"Sure, but—"

"Look. What with this?" She was pointing to another underlined quotation. It was a description of Nick Carraway's love interest: "Jordan Baker instinctively avoided clever shrewd men and now I saw that this was because she felt safer on a plane where any divergence from a code would be thought impossible. She was incurably dishonest.

She wasn't able to endure being at a disadvantage, and given this unwillingness I suppose she had begun dealing in subterfuges when she was very young in order to keep that cool insolent smile turned to the world and yet satisfy the demands of her hard jaunty body.

It made no difference to me. Dishonesty in a woman is a thing you never blame deeply."

"This is other woman. With same things as man. See? And then at end, there is very good line from Jordan: 'It take two to make an accident.' Is true, I think much true, in book—with Tom and lady, Gatsby, Daisy, all of it."

I sat down and typed. Soon we had come to the end of the fifth page of a five-page paper without having written a conclusion. I read the last sentences aloud. Yelizaveta nodded as she agreed or shook her head as she disagreed and we hit the middle of a sixth page and her paper was written.

"Why don't you look it over," I said.

Yelizaveta took the paper and gave it a cursory glance and handed it back. She was too busy looking at the CD tower pushed up against the wall next to her. Since I'd received a bulky black Sony Discman for my Bar Mitzvah years earlier I'd spent my money on all the CDs I could get my hands on. Yelizaveta was turned from me and rifling through the columns of CDs, pulling them out of their slots in the tower and opening jewel cases and thumbing through liner notes.

"Well, what'd you think of the paper?" I said.

"Is fine."

"You hardly even glanced at it."

"Don't need."

"Well why not?" I said.

"You did it. So it is good. Has to be."

I put down her paper and my pen and with a nascent untrammeled authority I kissed Yelizaveta's neck. I put my hand under her shirt again where the skin on her stomach moved away from my hand, then went calm. I tugged up on the bottom of her shirt with both hands. This was the first time I'd gotten naked with a girl, and it was clumsier than expected. Liza put her elbow directly down on the first draft of her paper so now it was hopelessly creased. I tossed it and took my shirt off. Now it was chest skin against chest skin. The hairs on my chest pulled against her bra strap.

I had left the window cracked when we smoked. It nipped at Yelizaveta's skin, which pulled itself into stippled bumps like waves on the ocean. The cold spread all over her face.

"It is much cold, too much. I don't have shirt."

"Then I'll go close it."

The wintersmell remained in the room. Yelizaveta held her shirt to the front of her chest. I grabbed her from behind and pressed her against my chest with my hand cupped over her breasts—and she let me. My mouth was overeager on her neck. She dropped her wrinkled shirt to the floor. Finally I got her bra off. She turned from me and lay down on my bed. Then she sat up with her hands on her thighs.

There was something violent in seeing her this way for the first time. Her left breast was slightly bigger than the right. The space between her hips and her shoulders was a bit too long, making her body appear disproportionate in a way that made me aroused and nauseated. I started to wish she would never look at me again. I couldn't tell if I wanted her to leave, or if I wanted to grab her, or if I wanted to cover her with blankets and swaddle her like an infant.

"We watch movie," Yelizaveta said. I'd undone my belt. My thumb and forefinger were unbuttoning my jeans. "*Beauty and Beast*," she said. It seemed a silly thing to say with one's shirt off. We put on *Beauty and the Beast*. I came back to the bed. My shirt was off. I wanted to cover up, to start over, but my pants were half-open. Yelizaveta finished unbuttoning me, her bare nipple hard and dry against my thumb. She reached into my boxers and wrapped her fingers around me very tightly, but it wasn't tight enough. She moved her cold hand much faster than I would have. I reached down and pressed my fingers against her through her pants.

Yelizaveta shoved my hand off with her upper arm. Then she got off the bed, turned her body around, and got down on her knees. But before she got there, I'd started to go. My whole body went tense with embarrassment and joy and embarrassment and concentric circles of pleasure ran across my arms and torso. I closed my eyes. My hands were down to my sides, very tight to my body.

I wanted to be alone, but Yelizaveta only held me tighter in her hand. Then she took me out of her mouth and pressed her thumb against the head and it was like being tickled too hard. Yelizaveta kept on going. I tried to pull her up but she pushed me away again. I was still refracting paroxysms of release in her bottom hand, but the rubbing from her other thumb was too much. It filled me with a sensation two octaves too high.

Finally she pulled away and cleared some hairs from her mouth. She started to hum along with the movie very quietly. Then she got up and tried to kiss me. I kept my mouth closed.

"What is this?" she said.

She let go of me. I felt a desire I hadn't had with her before, like an alarm was going off in the back of my head.

"You should rinse your mouth out first."

"What is it!" she said.

Now she licked me across the lips. She wrapped her fingers back around me and the alarm stopped ringing.

We kissed for a long time. Yelizaveta had a gentler nature than I'd expected. She kissed mostly with her lips, rarely with her tongue, and she ran her long fingernails along my back. The star tattoo on her chest changed color in the mint television light, going from green to aqua to a dark, dark blue with the bright Disney colors of the movie. The wintersmell was all over her skin.

\*

"I am thinking about it," Dmitri said. He'd just gotten in my car. "For a very long time there is something I want to do in Baltimore." He pulled a small, sweaty roll of twenties out of his pocket. He thumbed through it and then stashed it again.

I didn't know what we were going to buy, and it seemed that Dmitri could sense my apprehension when we got in my car at the end of the day. I'd bought bags before, but I'd certainly never driven into the city for them. He said that his friends sometimes cruised West Baltimore, but he assured me that he himself never joined.

"If I am to be writer or politician," Dmitri said, "I cannot corrupt my brain with these things. If I am to see beauty of world, I must see it through pure eyes."

He wasn't kidding.

"Mystics have always used drugs," I said.

"When I am first learning English," Dmitri said as I drove us out of Pikesville, "my grandfather has to have gallbladder removed. They gave him anesthetics to knock him out. My English tutor taught me word in English. 'Are anesthetics they'll use,' he said. I said, as we'd just been studying vocabulary to get into good school, 'Is similar to "aesthetics?"' And my teacher tells me, 'Yes, is very good thing. You are understanding. Etymology.' 'So why does my grandfather need anesthetic?' I ask my English tutor. He said, 'So he will feel nothing.' My grandfather feel nothing instead of pain. But I do not have pain now. So I don't want to feel nothing. I want to feel everything. Would Alyosha Karamazov have needed pill or to smoke to make him see God? Of course not. Neither do I."

"But your friends go down to West Baltimore, right?"

"Yes. I go with them and make sure they do nothing stupid. Is very dangerous place, West Baltimore."

Just before the Baltimore city line there is a long stretch of Falls Road where the verdant stands of deciduous trees of Baltimore County thin—the road crosses a highway overpass, and an urban area approaches. My beige Volvo passed under the highway there. Alongside the road Dmitri spied a broken-down Chevy in an otherwise empty parking lot.

"You stop here," he said. We slowed and pulled into the lot. The old Impala had been stripped. It was only a dimpled scarred old frame.

"What a beat-up piece of shit," I said.

"Looks like one my father drives."

"Drives?"

"I don't know what father drives now. He did not come with us because he is learning to become petroleum geologist."

"A petroleum geologist?"

"My father make money in business. But now is not good. Now he will work at big oil plant. In Astrakhan, where my family is from. He says he will make so much money to bring to us and we will move from Baltimore to New York City."

Dmitri bent down next to the Chevy. Underneath the car, oil had collected black and viscous in the patches of white snow. Just in front of us a small pool of water had collected, no more than a glass-full. Oil emulsified atop the water. Dmitri made to put his finger into it.

"Hey," I said.

But Dmitri just put his finger down into the water again. The oil refracted the mid-afternoon sunlight, the vermillion, yellow and crimson patterns of the oil chasing after each other as if to bite the other's tail. We crouched and watched for a minute and the water and oil stopped moving. Dmitri put his fingers in some snow beside him. He rubbed it between his fingers, then put his fingers to his nose.

"You are right to try and stop me," Dmitri said. "My fingers smell of oil now. But look what you have seen! Not much, but then very much." He wiped his hand on his jeans. "My grandfather told us of many bad things he hear when he is in gulag," Dmitri said. "But he always say they did not ever even hear enough of what was happening in Europe to know Nazis were so bad. He did not talk like American might, be made to feel good for bad experiences he has. He felt everything, like man. In gulag, people do not treat my grandfather well. Vory v Zakonye are gangsters. There is scar on grandfather's face, on cheek from it. When I was boy I touched scar. 'Is kind of person you stay away from,' my grandfather says. 'Instead you will have power from brain.'"

At Fell's Point, Dmitri and I walked up South Broadway, Ann Street, then with a newfound sense of purpose all the way up to Fleet Street to a tattoo parlor. There were designs displayed all along the windows outside. A girl with a thin silver bar through her nose was sitting with her elbow propped on her knee. She was smoking a cigarette. She scowled at me. Then she saw Dmitri.

"Our little Russian returns," she said. "You got money this time?"

"I have money, Genessa. You have star?"

While we stood in the entrance to the parlor, the tattoo artist flipped through a pile of drawings until she came upon what she was looking for. She held it out in front of her. On the page was a simple star, like an icon you might find on an old map: five points, with deep blue shadings on half of each point.

"Is it exactly," Dmitri said.

"Well let's do it. You want a shot or something first? I've got some Old Crow in back."

"I do not want to have thing come between me and feeling! If I am to have tattoo, I am to feel it when it is done."

"You're hardcore, guy," the girl said. She sat Dmitri down in a chair. He handed Genessa the grimy roll of twenties. Dmitri unbuttoned his shirt and pulled his arms out of the sleeves. He had a squiggle of hair at the middle of his chest, but otherwise his skin was the exact color of his sister's. "It'll just be like you're getting stung by bees, by a whole bunch of bees," the tattoo artist said. "Let me know if you need me to stop."

For the next hour and a half the tattoo artist leaned over Dmitri's chest with her whirring metal pen and dug ink into his chest. At first Dmitri gritted his teeth. Then a line of sweat began to glisten on his forehead. As it drew down to his eyes, I expected him to ask Genessa to stop. But he didn't. The sweat on Dmitri's brow left a steady gleam. Only once, the tattoo artist stopped to wipe some sweat from her own brow. When she looked up to see Dmitri's face, she took a white rag from the counter and wiped his forehead for him. Just as she was getting near done—I could see now the shiny blue markings permeating Dmitri's skin—the flesh on Dmitri's face flicked a bit with the discomfort he was feeling. It wasn't a grimace, exactly, but more a flicking of the skin around his eyes and in his cheeks like a horse flicking off flies. He evinced no other discomfort.

When she finished, we walked back toward the harbor. I figured Dmitri wanted to check the thing out—I know I did—but it was cold and he was wearing a jacket, and if he was itching to see the tattoo it didn't show. Sunlight crept to the bottom of the squat buildings and colored facades of the row houses up and down Shakespeare Street. The air grew thin and cold. Once-luminous buildings now loomed above us like dark craggy mountain peaks.

"We can go home now," Dmitri said.

On our way out of the city I drove around downtown and over to Ft. McHenry. There was a long line of bunkers. Some were preserved, though most of them were newly built reproductions of the buildings that quartered US soldiers during the Revolutionary War. I told Dmitri we should see some of our local war history.

"So they say that right there—" I was pointing to an area between mounds reaching down toward the harbor from where we were standing—"right there is where Francis Scott Key was holed up when he wrote the National Anthem."

"The wars I know of are wars my grandfather fights in siege at Stalingrad against Nazis." I thought of the obtuse way my grandfather always mentioned the war but never talked about it. I said my grandfather had fought in World War II as well. Dmitri asked what he did.

"Well, he's a survivor," I said.

"From Auschwitz?"

"He's Hungarian and he was—he was in a camp."

"Death camp?"

I didn't know. I'd never listened or asked. Dmitri walked back toward the car. It was late enough that I was ready to get home, so instead of the back way up Falls Road, this time I took us on I-83 to the Beltway. He turned to look outside his window. This new route back left only the backs of buildings—office buildings, prisons and factories—for us to look at. It was as if they'd all lifted their skirts as not to sully them, picked up their heels and turned away from the highway that had cut into the center of their row.

# FIVE

April arrived all misty and petulant and it was clear that the more Yelizaveta's annoyance grew over my not having invited her to dinner, the more difficult it would be finally to have her. I considered asking, but my mother beat me to it. One day that week she said, "Grandpa's coming for Passover."

"Really?"

"He wants to come for first Seder. First one since Grandma died."

My grandfather had never spent a Jewish holiday with us before. He and my grandmother had converted to Catholicism during the war, and never during my grandmother's life had he expressed any interest in coming for Seder.

"Do you want to see if Tanya is busy?" my mother said. "Or that other girl? That Elizabeta girl?"

So I invited Yelizaveta to dinner at our house, for Seder. I asked Dmitri to come, too. I did not invite Tanya to Seder. I didn't have to.

"So," my mother said later that evening. "Tanya called earlier, and she said she would love to come for Seder."

"She what?"

"Her parents decided last minute to go down to Boca for Seder with her grandparents. She has to stick around Pikesville for a tennis match."

"And how will she end up here?"

"I invited her, Sam. Did you not want to have her?"

"You didn't want to ask me if it was OK for her to come?"

"She's your oldest friend. Why wouldn't it be OK?"

"You just should've asked."

"OK, sorry. But you know, honey, you can never discount the importance of old friends. Tanya's family."

"It's more complicated than that."

"How so?"

"It just is. You didn't tell Tanya Yelizaveta was coming, did you?"

"I did."

My mother didn't seem nearly as distraught over it as I'd have liked her to be. She could be doting; now here she was after a catastrophe, barely reacting.

*

During that period I had just one thought in my head, and that thought had nothing to do with my best friend. What I thought of, to the exclusion of nearly everything else, was how things could be with Yelizaveta. The kinds of thoughts you might properly call fantasies. She was almost my girlfriend—that's what I believed, anyway.

One afternoon at lunch I saw Yelizaveta at a table with Fy and Benny. I'd never even thought of sitting with those guys before, but this time I picked up my lunch and joined them.

I said what's up. Liza said, "Is Dmitri friend from gym class. Is Samuel."

I said what's up again, this time nodding at them both.

Fy and Benny looked at each other. A minute later they picked up their lunches and left. Yelizaveta and I were alone now, sitting next to each other on the bench of the long cafeteria table—next to each other instead of across from each other. I had the idea that maybe Yelizaveta would turn and straddle the bench and, in essence, be straddling me.

Yelizaveta didn't turn to straddle the bench. She just looked down at her slim grey hamburger and took another bite.

I looked around to see if anyone was watching. But it was late in the day, and no one was really left. Which you would think would have made it less awkward when I turned and straddled the bench myself, right next to her.

"What do you do?" she said.

"Nothing," I said. But I didn't move back. I went to hold her hand. It was kind of slimy with grey hamburger. "Just holding your hand."

"Is weird time to hold hand," Yelizaveta said. A shock of embarrassment struck down through my palms. Just more than a month earlier we'd been naked together in my bedroom. I turned and put both of my legs under the table.

"So," I said. "I guess I'll see you soon or something?"

"We come to your house for Seder," Yelizaveta said. "In next week."

I said that yes, they would. I didn't want to be the one to have to leave, and so I watched her finish her burger. She did it quickly, and with a precision that swelled my throat closed with longing. Then she stood, and she reached down and kissed me on the cheek. It was a little bit of a greasy kiss, but warm: a pickaxe to the icy river that had frozen between us. By the time it occurred to me to stand up and reciporicate, she was already walking away.

\*

My grandfather arrived the afternoon of Seder. It was three o'clock. He had come down by train. I wondered what he did with his mind during all those hours alone. All that sitting and thinking. It had been just more than three months since we'd seen him up at his house in Wantagh, over Christmas break, but when he came through the door I saw my grandfather had been through a transformation you might only find in Ovid. He must have lost thirty pounds. Where there had been bags protruding under his eyeballs and above his cheekbones, now there was loose skin that sunk in toward the socket. His cheekbones stuck out like craggy rock formations. His skin was weary and jaundiced.

"Samuel," he said. "This is the first time I come to your house for Passover." He held my face between his thumb and index finger, each of which passed over my face like they were covered in burlap. He bent and kissed my cheek, his face rubbing against mine with wiry bristles. In the past I would have taken off for my room until dinner—now I found myself longing to find out what had changed my grandfather, who I didn't suspect was capable of change. But Grandpa said he needed a nap, tired from the train, and my mother showed him up to the guest room.

When the doorbell rang it was Yelizaveta. She was wearing a white dress that extended just down to her mid-thigh and at the top pulled down off her shoulder. She had brought a box of macaroons. Though my parents did not keep kosher the rest of the year, our house was kept quite carefully pesadek, and only macaroons were allowed for the week. I wondered who'd told Liza that this was the appropriate dessert.

"You're early," I said.

She kissed me on the cheek.

"Where's Dmitri?" I said.

"He comes late," she said.

Yelizaveta walked into the living room. My grandfather had arisen from his nap and now sat in front of the television. From the doorway to the room, where we stood, we could see only the crown of his bald head.

"I am Yelizaveta," Yelizaveta said.

My grandfather's head did not move.

"Grandpa," I said.

He didn't move. I shook him awake. He grunted and stood.

"Hallo," he said. He tottered about, looking as if his legs had recently been replaced by a new pair a couple of inches longer.

"I am grandfather, Imre," he said. This was the first time any of my friends had ever met my grandfather, whose thick accent and broken English had only ever embarrassed me before. Yelizaveta put her hand out to him. He reached for her shoulders to give her a kiss on each cheek.

"I'm going to take Yelizaveta into the kitchen, Grandpa," I said. In the kitchen, my mother continued basting her brisket while I introduced Yelizaveta.

"Is very nice meets you," Yelizaveta said.

My mother said, "Oh, welcome, Yelizaveta. We'll start soon. Come on in."

The doorbell rang again. The neighbors from the end of the block, the Weinbergs, had arrived with their two young boys.

"And is this your new friend your mother has been talking about?" Mrs. Weinberg said. Yelizaveta stood there without speaking. She didn't care about Mrs. Weinberg, and she wasn't going to pretend. I showed Mrs. Weinberg in. I was just finished hanging her coat when Tanya arrived.

"Oh, hey Tanya," I said. No one else said anything. Yelizaveta stood by the doorway with her shoulders square to Tanya.

"This is Yelizaveta, Dmitri's sister," I said. "You know Dmitri, my friend from gym."

"Of course," Tanya said. "Take my coat now, would you, Sam?"

Yelizaveta showed my grandfather in from the living room. She sat him in a chair next to mine. On my side of the table were myself and Yelizaveta. Tanya had no choice but to sit down on the other side. Next to her was an empty chair and two glasses of wine—one for Eliahu Ha-Navi, Elijah the Prophet, for whom we left the back door open, and the other for Dmitri Abramovitch, the guest, for whom we left the front unlocked.

"This is the Matzah," my father said. "It is unleavened because there wasn't time enough. This is the Maror," my father said. "We eat it to commemorate the bitterness." The horseradish went around the table. When it landed in front of my grandfather he interrupted my father's davening.

"I did not found any more of this," he said. My father looked up.

"What did he say?"

"I did not found any more of this—how you say?"

"How do I say what? Fifty years in this country and he still hasn't learned the language."

"What this is called, Samuel?"

"He wants more horseradish," I said.

The skin around my father's collar was turning the color of borscht.

"There's not anymore, Ок?" my father said.

"I'll take care of it," I said. But just then the doorbell rang. Dmitri pounded on the door again before I could open it.

"I am sorry I arrive so late," Dmitri said. His over-large suit hung off him like elephant skin.

"The door was unlocked," I said. My father had continued through the service while Dmitri entered.

"Samuel, would you like to say the Four Questions for us? I believe you're the youngest in the room," he said.

"This is Dmitri, Yelizaveta's brother," I said.

Dmitri raised his arm to greet everyone. He sat down.

"Samuel," my father said.

"Actually," Dmitri said, "I am youngest. Yes? I have been just learning in Hebrew classes these past years how to say Four Questions and this would be my first chance," he said. "I have never even been to Seder before."

The Weinburgs looked at each other and nodded— a young man taking seriously his Judaism was sure to be OK. I looked at my father. My father looked at Dmitri. My father looked at me and nodded.

So Dmitri sang the questions: "Ma nish tanah, ha lialah hazeh, mi cole ha layla, mi cole ha layla, ha lialah hazeh, ha lialah hazeh, mi cole ha layla" and on and on. His pronunciation was markedly Slavic and his Hebrew wasn't perfect, but it was good. As with everything he did, he was just so earnest. The Weinbergs nodded to each other again. When Dmitri finished my father took the service back up.

"Now we take the third cup of wine," my father said. He raised the cup. "Baruch ata adoni, elohenu melech ha'olam, asher, kidishanu, vikiemanu, boreh piree, ha'gofen," he said. We all drank the third cup. Tanya, Dmitri, Yelizaveta and I downed ours. All this time my grandfather had not said a word. When we read from the Haggadah we passed our way around the table and read aloud from the English translations. My father, Tanya, and the Weinbergs read from the Hebrew parts at times, though my father davened most of the Hebrew. But each time any of these duties came around to my grandfather he simply shook his head. It went along to the next reader until halfway through the Seder it became clear that he wasn't going to read at all. We simply skipped him.

My father had already explained what each aspect of the Seder meant even before it came up officially in the Haggadah so he spent the next half hour davening the part of the service in which God is exalted for delivering our people from harm. I kept looking at my grandfather, but his face evinced no reaction. We were almost to the end of the Haggadah, only a couple more minutes of prayer and reminiscing left. My father read: "Leshana haba bi' Yerushalayim!"

The sweet smell of gefilte fish and horseradish filled the room, commingling with the rich aroma of brisket. My father had gotten up and put on some low solo guitar music in the other room.

"Do you still play with the guitar?" my grandfather said.

"I don't anymore."

"Did your girlfriend ever played an instrument?" my grandfather said.

Yelizaveta didn't hear him.

"My grandfather wants to know if you ever played an instrument," I said.

"I did," Yelizaveta said. "I play piano four years. But father say if I ride horsebacks he will sell it. I like riding horsebacks. I am twelve and he sells it. He not want me to ride horses, and he threatens to sells it, and he sells it."

"Very sad," my grandfather said. "I did loved the horses when I am a boy. Magyar men were known for their horse-riding, yes?"

Yelizaveta appeared too caught up in her anger at the memory of the piano and the horse to respond. She kept trying to butter her matzah.

"You came from Hungary when war ended?" Dmitri said.

"We come to New York from Budapest many years ago," he said.

"You survived war? Samuel say you are survivor."

My grandfather fiddled with his napkin. His gaze dropped to the tablecloth.

"We did comes through from Budapest to New York in 1956. But before this, I am in labor camp, and mother is in Budapest ghetto."

"My grandfather survived war in gulag."

"I am in labor camp," my grandfather said. "One what is called Rimaszombat, in Ukraine."

"And what happened there?" Dmitri said.

"Rimaszombat—this is forced labor camp," he said. "This is the forced labor camp. I do work there—shoveling work, work on roads and all this. Men in the Labor Service don't do the Army things, just helps out with what they has to. Later the Germans come, there is not so much resistance."

"My grandfather lives in gulag until he gets out," Dmitri said. "It was hard. It must be hard in labor camp in Ukraine, if they make you help Germans."

"Is no Jewish helping Germans!" my grandfather said. "Hungarian Jewish are put into forced labor camp!"

I'd never seen my grandfather respond so acerbically toward anyone. He was always the peacemaker. What else had changed now that my grandmother was gone?

"This is not what I mean," Dmitri said.

"So what do you mean?" I said.

"I was only in Labor Service early in the war," my grandfather said. "This camp is north of Budapest. I left the labor camp and did come to Budapest."

"How did you survive?" Dmitri said.

Grandpa's hands were clutched together on the table. He said nothing. His thin lower lip drew in toward his teeth. He was struggling.

"I have false papers. Like lots of Jewish. We survive."

"My grandfather said he was lucky to be in gulag. He lives there while his brother and father die in siege at Stalingrad. So some of one in labor camps were lucky," Dmitri said.

We both looked at him now. He still just clutched his hands. His eyelids fluttered a bit when he blinked. His lower lip drew even tighter and he stopped looking at Dmitri. Now he looked at me, his eyelids still fluttering. I could see sweat on the top of his head. Tanya and Yelizaveta were listening. My father, too, had stopped his conversation.

"Will you pass this thing?" He was pointing at the charoset. "With the apples and the cinnamon," he said. "Is very good."

That was the end of his story: a request for apples and cinnamon and horseradish.

\*

Once the plates were cleared and everyone had finished eating, there was a moment that might have been the most hopeful of that whole year. Dmitri was in the kitchen helping my mother load plates into the dishwasher; Tanya was helping too. My father had taken Dmitri's seat at the dining room table. He and my grandfather were talking about the latter's return to Long Island and while the two rarely showed each other affection, here they were talking train schedules like they were conspiring on some elaborate plot. My father called across the table to ask if I would take my grandfather to the train station the following afternoon.

Yelizaveta and I talked about how we would take a drive out to Meadowbrook Park later in the week. Then my father broke off his conversation with my grandfather and said, "Time for the afikomen!" He went off to hide the middle matzah, then returned a couple minutes later to the dining room and sent the kids after it.

Everyone returned to the dining room from the kitchen. The Weinberg kids went to seek out the afikomen. Conversation lifted back up in the room like an orchestra tuning. Presently there was a banging of doors out in the hallway. The youngest of the children came in with the afikomen in his hand.

"What've you got there?" Mr. Weinberg said. The little Weinberg awaited his prize. My father gave him a five-dollar bill. Mr. Weinberg gave him a ten. Soon after, the Weinbergs expressed their thanks and left.

"I'm gonna go now, too," Tanya said.

"No—let us all hang out for some time," Dmitri said.

Tanya was already standing and getting ready to go but now she stopped. She shifted from one foot to the other. Her teeth were purpled with wine.

"Stay," Dmitri said. "Yelizaveta and I would like to hang out."

Yelizaveta just continued to pick the polish off her nails. Dmitri looked at me.

"We go to your room and meet you there." He took Yelizaveta up the stairs. Tanya and I were alone.

"Actually, there's a party over at Pinetops," Tanya said. "At Mandy Horowitz's. We should go. You haven't been out in a long time. We could catch up on the ride."

"And what am I supposed to do with my guests?"

"They can come, Samuel, if you want them to. Maybe they'd want to come to the party."

"I'm gonna stay here."

"And then meet me at the party later?"

"I told Yelizaveta that I'd hang out with her later. It'd be rude to leave."

"You're right," Tanya said. "I guess it would be. Rude. I'll see you later, Samuel."

I went upstairs to my room where Dmitri and Yelizaveta were already smoking a cigarette at my window. "You don't have to worry," Dmitri said. "We know to keep smoke in house, so yours parents don't kick us out. We are friends. We do not get you in trouble. You do not have to tell me this."

"I wouldn't ever hurt either of you guys," I said. The Manishevitz had brought out a certain sentimental side in me. For Dmitri, it kept him mostly unchanged.

"I know!" Dmitri said. He looked over at his sister. She'd just turned around, having ditched the smoke, and had gone to sit on the couch. "I know you are good! You do not have to convince me of things now."

"What do you talk?" Yelizaveta said. "Is about me?"

"Samuel and I are saying how is nice, all of us together, and we don't get in trouble for smoke."

Yelizaveta shrugged and put her cigarettes back in her pocket. After we'd talked for a while—I showed them how to play *Super Mario Brothers* on my Nintendo—Yelizaveta said she had to go; a friend was coming to get her. I asked her where she was going, but she just said, "I goes now." I didn't give it a second thought. Dmitri and I smoked a couple more cigarettes. We talked about *The Idiot*. I'd finally read it, and he illuminated what he felt were the particularly sensualist parts of Rogozhin's fiery behavior and Prince Myshkin's responses. Mostly I listened. We talked into the small hours of the night.

Finally Dmitri said he'd better leave. I walked him downstairs and closed the door firmly behind him, making sure that if Elijah the Prophet was inside the house, he would stay in, and if he was out, he would stay out.

# SIX

Tanya asked me to meet her at Weiss's the next day. When I arrived, she was eating from a paper carton full of french fries. Some old bluehaired women sat at a table nearby, both wearing the same pair of baby blue old woman pants, the kind with a high elastic waist and big thick cuffs at bottom.

"Want one?" Tanya said.

"Just ate," I said.

"I have to tell you something. And it's not easy." She put her fingers into her fries and dragged three of them through a swirl of ketchup she'd smeared on a napkin. "Last night I went to that party over at Mandy Horowitz's. Mandy's parents had gone out of town and everybody was there." She wiped her fingers on a napkin, looking at them to make sure they were clean. "I talked with Mandy and some of those girls."

I picked one of her fries from off her plate. I smothered it in ketchup and ate it. While she'd started out uncharacteristically shy, I could see Tanya settle into herself as she started to tell the story.

"While I was talking to Mandy she was like, 'Did you hear about Jeremy Goldstein?' I figured she was talking about the fight from months back, so I was just like, 'Yeah—old news.' And Mandy's friend Julie was there and she looked at me like I didn't know what I was talking about, so I said, 'Oκ, maybe not.' And Mandy said, 'I hear he's been hooking up with that Russian girl.' Just to be completely clear I said, 'What Russian girl?' Mandy said, 'You know, that girl Sam Gerson's dating. That Yelizaveta girl.'"

"Bullshit," I said.

The bluehairs looked over and narrowed their bovine eyes.

"Just let me finish, Oκ? I said the same thing you did. I liked Yelizaveta last night. And you're Sam Gerson, so I was pissed. I said the same thing you did—fuck that, Sam's been hooking up with that girl. Those girls just looked at each other like before. And before they could say more, I went looking for Goldstein. I was pissed for you. I went upstairs and opened a bedroom door and Sam, I know you're gonna think I'm lying. You're gonna hate me for telling you. It just happened."

"What happened?" I said. The bluehairs were moving so slowly it made you want to go over and smash their sandwiches into their faces. One of them turned to look at me.

"It was Goldstein and Yelizaveta."

I didn't say anything.

"It's true, Sam. I wouldn't even have told you if it was just a rumor."

"Fuck that."

"It's not just gossip, Sam."

"Yelizaveta and Dmitri stayed around my house after Seder."

"What time did they leave?"

"I don't know," I said. "I wasn't keeping fucking time on my plans last night. Midnight?"

"It was easily three before I left the party, Samuel," Tanya said.

"Actually, Dmitri left late," I said. "Yelizaveta left earlier because a friend was picking her up. But she was getting a ride home."

Tanya wouldn't lift her eyes, though just a minute before she'd been looking at me the whole time.

"Fuck that," I said. "Why would you go so far to try and make me hate her."

"Samuel, what are you talking about? Don't be a jerk."

"Maybe that's just what I am now," I said. The air in the room was turning to some kind of noxious gas burning my eyes. I wanted to rub them but I couldn't have lifted my arms if I tried. We were breathing it deeper and deeper.

"There's one more thing. I had to tell you because I bitched Yelizaveta out."

"What do you mean?"

"The door had been open long enough for me to see who it was, so I told Yelizaveta that I was gonna tell you, that after you had her over to Seder what bullshit it was she was cheating on you. Goldstein told me to get out and I did, because, frankly, he was really pissed and he's big and he scares me."

"That's just a load of bullshit," I heard myself say. "I'm supposed to believe that Yelizaveta left my house last night after coming to Seder at my parents' house and hanging out with me and her brother in my bedroom and went to a party to hook up with Jeremy Goldstein?"

"I don't understand the way you've been acting, Sam. I mean, what do you think?"

"What do I think? I think you know even if I just ask Yelizaveta if it's true, she'll be pissed I even suspected her. That'll be it with us."

"You actually believe I'm that manipulative?"

"I don't know."

"I thought you would want to know."

"You wanted to be the one to tell."

"Not to hurt you. Seriously—you think I'm that manipulative?" Tanya pushed on the side of her Dr. Brown's. The can made a little crinkling sound. "That's insane." She was still remarkably composed. "That's insane."

"So's your story."

The bluehairs left the deli; a whiff of early spring came into the room. The wind had pushed a cloud off the sun, and suddenly the early afternoon light filled the place with the most cloying hue. Light reflected off every surface in Weiss's.

"I guess I'll just have to talk to her," I said.

"I don't care what you do."

The acid we had been breathing was now a liquid coursing through my veins. My mind hit up against the reality of confronting Yelizaveta. Tanya was still sitting across from me. Two new bluehairs came in. The air-conditioned air again vacated the place and left us smelling the same spring wind.

"I gotta go," I said.

And I did.

\*

When I got home I planned to go directly for the telephone. But in the living room I found my father and my grandfather waiting for me. Grandpa was set to leave. I was supposed to take him to the train station and here he was, ready to go. He shifted from one foot to the other. He'd not left Wantagh since my grandmother died and it wore on him. He was so gaunt.

"Back just in time," my father said. "You ready to take Grandpa?"

"I am ready to go, Samuel," my grandfather said. His eyes welled up with tears that might have been spurred by happiness at having been with his family. But they seemed somehow too plentiful.

"Glad you could be here," my father said. It appeared they might hug, but they didn't. They both just stood there. I used the awkward silence that followed to jump in.

"Dad?" I said. "What if you took Grandpa? I'm just in the middle of something."

"What could you be in the middle of that's more important than your grandfather?" he said.

Grandpa looked at me.

"Yeah. You're right. Sorry. I've got nothing."

We took the highway to the train station. I'd never before driven with such frustrated purpose. All the way out of the suburbs a line of sound barriers was being built along the Beltway, next to the gated communities of Pikesville. My classmates' wealthy parents had lobbied hard to have these walls erected to muffle the tiresome drone of traffic that came through the short stands of trees into their backyards. I'd been in those neighborhoods—Goldstein himself lived in Arbor Estates, one of the gated communities on just the other side of those barriers—and I knew now how much quieter they were than, say, Dmitri's backyard, only the hushed hum of traffic vibrating innocuously on the other side. How fast would a car have to travel to pass through those barriers and drive the outside world violently into those secluded backyards? Out on the highway my grandfather and I ground along amidst the bestial traffic groan.

"What is it, these big walls?" my grandfather said. He had seen how I was staring at them instead of the road.

"Bullshit soundproofing."

"How is this?"

"So that there won't be all the noise from the highways coming through to those houses. So they can be in control of their destiny and everyone else's," I said. "Those people do whatever they want and get these walls built."

My grandfather looked at me. Then he looked out the window again.

"You have so much hate for these sound things?" my grandfather said. "Is a hard thing to hate."

"I hate all this bullshit." I rolled my window up. The car filled with grandfather smell, naphthalene and stale Kool cigarette smoke. He was a very small man now that he'd lost all that weight. The acid in my veins started to drain. My arms didn't feel strong enough to steer.

"You seemed to like Yelizaveta, Grandpa," I said.

"She is very beautiful. When I was a boy in Hungary, I did kissed many girls like this. I was good with the women."

"Apparently I'm not so good with women."

"This is not true! I see how this girl does look at you, Samuel. Your grandfather is good with women, your father is good with women, you will be good with women." He was saying all the things a grandfather should say to boost his grandson's ego. "Your grandmother was the most beautiful in Budapest."

"Yeah," I said. "Grandpa, did you ever have to deal with a woman who—well, who had another man when you were with her?"

"Another?" my grandfather said.

"Like, I don't know, I guess not cheating on you. But maybe."

"There was always many women, Sammycom! This is the first thing. But then there was grandmother. You are married, you be careful of your wife, she never leave. But until then! You are with the woman, your friend are with the woman, you do all this and not to worry."

"Right," I said. "But, I mean. Really? That seems like bullshit. I mean—sorry. What if the other guy isn't your friend? He's just, you know, someone you played baseball with and you don't really like him anyway?"

"Not a friend? The other man should always be your friend, Sammycom. Does it matter, you don't like him? You see this when you become older. It is enough time that there is men that isn't your friend. There is war, there is army against you—then he can't be your friend. But you are American, I am American, he is American, yes? We are all the friend, yes? We should all be the friend."

It sounded like such a nice, pure sentiment. I wished it were true.

"Maybe. But maybe he's just some asshole who wants what you've got, though."

"This did happen to you?"

"I have to find out."

Soon the sound barriers fell away. We were nearing the city. Just after the barriers stopped, it was easy to look through at the backyards of houses on the other side, the houses in neighborhoods where residents didn't hold the sway to have sound barriers erected, where the roar of traffic came unhindered through the thin futile stands of conifers at the backs of the yards. Then we were in the city. Along the highway ran the tops of countless buildings, a few scattered smokestacks, the big old Domino Sugar sign in neon lights.

When we arrived at the train station I said goodbye to my grandfather. I handed him his bag. I stood and watched for far less time than I should have as he went in through the renovated front of the train station.

*

When I got back to our house I called Yelizaveta and she agreed to meet with me later that afternoon. I picked her up in Greenhill. We drove all the way out toward Towson without talking. She broke our silence.

"Where do we go?"

"What do you mean?"

"We just drive for now. Do we go somewhere?"

"I guess we're just going to do whatever you want to."

"OK, is fine then."

It seemed she didn't understand I was trying to get at her.

"Is fine, is how I like it," she said. "Then we go Meadowbrook Park. I like it there."

When we reached the state park I pulled up through the drive and past the main parking lot. We drove a couple of miles down a road where I would sometimes go to smoke pot. I pulled over and didn't get out of the car.

"So I have to ask you about something, and I don't know if it's true or what. Tanya told me something, and I want to think it isn't true. Don't think I'm accusing you, but I have to ask. About you and Jeremy."

"Goldstein," Yelizaveta said.

"I heard you were hooking up with him after you left my house the other night." We still hadn't looked at each other. Though the car was no longer moving, we both continued to look forward. My hands were still on the wheel. "Is it true?"

"Is true?" Yelizaveta said.

"Yeah, I'm asking. Is it true that Tanya caught you hooking up with Jeremy Goldstein?"

Yelizaveta reached down and unbuckled her seatbelt. She turned and faced me.

"Is true." I didn't reach to unbuckle my belt. "You are angry," she said.

"I'm angry? Yeah, I'm angry. You and I had, I thought, I thought we had something going. I've been helping, and we're. I just kind of. That we. I loved you." Now there was really no sound in the car at all. "Fuck," I said.

I unbuckled my seatbelt, threw the driver's side door open and got out. Loamy muddy leaves ground under the heels of my sneakers. They'd been covered by snow all winter long. I tromped along, waiting to hear Yelizaveta call after me to stop. Fifty yards up I slowed. Yelizaveta wasn't following me—she hadn't even gotten out of the car. The next thing I heard were tires spinning against wet leaves. Mud and entropy kicked back and the car swung out into the path. It backed up after lurching to a stop. The car went forward again and Yelizaveta, who to the best of my knowledge had never before even tried to drive a car, completed an expert three-point turn and drove off. The whole time I just stood and watched. Now I was alone in the woods, miles from civilization.

Ten minutes later I was sitting on the side of the road when my Volvo came back up the path. Yelizaveta pulled up next me. She made no move to reach across and roll down my window. I opened the door.

"You gets in Volvo car now," Yelizaveta said.

"I can drive my own car." My Volvo lurched forward a foot. The frame of the door slammed into my shoulder.

"You gets in now, please." So I got into the shotgun seat of my own car. For someone I believed had never driven before, Liza was quite impressive.

"You're actually kind of good," I said.

"Lessons."

"Dmitri's friends?"

"Jeremy lets me drive father's car. Is Mercedes. Is nice car. Fast."

"Are you fucking kidding me?"

"Kidding fucking?" Yelizaveta said.

"I don't even know what that means," I said. "I mean—you've been getting driving lessons from Goldstein, too?"

I'd never even thought of letting her drive my car. Yelizaveta pushed down hard on the accelerator and the automatic transmission hadn't up-shifted yet. The engine revved a warning.

"We are just young," Yelizaveta said.

"Were you together with him before?"

"No 'together.'"

"But you'd hooked up?"

"It is nothing. 'It take two to make accident,' like Gatsby book say." She slowed down. The engine agreed with Yelizaveta. The transmission downshifted.

"So is that what Dmitri and his friends were fighting with Goldstein about back in the fall? Over you being with him?"

"Ya. But we are just young, and there is lot of time, lot of people."

"Things were going good, I thought. We were hanging out, and we only just really hooked up for the first time and…"

She slowed the car a bit more.

"This was all fun," she said. God, I wanted to touch her. The car ran smoothly. The woods outside my window seemed less imposing for the first time since we'd gotten into the car.

"So. So what's the problem?" I said.

"Is no problem. You are good, and I like it. Nothing change."

Now she slowed to a stop. She pulled over to the side of the road.

"Well, so what's this all mean?" I said. "No more Goldstein?"

"Does not mean it." Yelizaveta turned the car off and reached over to put her hand against the back of my neck. I had my hands clutched in my lap. Now they squeezed together more tightly. Yelizaveta took her hand off the back of my neck. The car was cooling, and with it rose a desperation for that hand to be on my neck again. So I kissed her and put my hand on her breast. She rubbed her hand against me. Then she unzipped my pants and slid her hand beneath my waistband. I did the same to her, and this time she let me.

It made a mess, but there were tissues in my glove box.

"So can I drive now?" I said.

Yelizaveta got out. I got out and we switched seats. When we got back to her house, Yelizaveta made to get out of the car.

"Wait a sec," I said. She stopped and looked at me.

"When will I see you again?"

"I have more paper to write."

My face was getting hot, so not knowing if I meant it but knowing for certain I would do it, I said I would be happy to help.

# SEVEN

When I arrived at Greenhill later that week the front door to the Zilbers' house was locked and no one responded to my knocking. It wasn't until I quit that I heard voices carrying around from the backyard. One of them was barking some orders over and over as I rounded to the back of the house. Then it stopped.

Benny Dudkin ran straight into my chest. My back hit the ground. There was a sharp pain in my coccyx. The football Benny was trying to catch landed on the ground next to us, bouncing along off of each of its pointed tips until it rolled to a stop next to me.

"Fuck goddamn!" Benny said. "I had this!" He brushed the cakes of mud off his hands and popped up from the grass. I got up from the grass, too.

"You fucking ran into me," I said.

"What the fuck you say?" Benny said. A corona of sun formed a fiery crown of orange curls over his head. I could see every black pore on his pale white nose.

"It's Oκ, it's Oκ," Dmitri said.

I backed off. Benny backed off. Fy Warchawski was standing at the other end of the backyard, ostensibly the quarterback of the pass play I'd broken up. Benny was still sneering at me. Dmitri gave me a hand off the ground. The sun nipped at my shoulders. The roar of cars on the highway on the other side of the backyard rose and fell.

"Liza around?" I said.

"She's gone," Dmitri said.

"With who?"

Dmitri cocked his head.

"How do I know?" he said. "I don't keep track. You would know more."

"Is good to see you," Fy said. His lats were so overdeveloped that his arms couldn't lay flat against his sides. Every time he grabbed my hand I wondered if his handshake didn't crush some of the metacarpals in my right hand. I squeezed back as hard as I could. The pain steeled my shoulders, and now some of the confidence I'd lost came back, but in a different strain. Instead of raising the Yelizaveta question, when Dmitri asked me to play with them, I played. Benny just squared his shoulders and treated me the same as the others.

I started hanging out with Dmitri, Benny and Fy a lot in the weeks that followed. We played on Tuesday and Friday afternoons. It would have been more fun to play with, say, six guys. But we only had the four of us. We played hard and when there was a chance to hit each other we took it. Usually as soon as the game was over I'd go home. But one afternoon a couple weeks into this routine, we all sat together in the grass until our breathing grew quiet.

"You know Liza's hooking up with Goldstein," I said to no one in particular.

"Again?" Benny said. "He don't learn from last time?"

Dmitri kept his mouth shut.

"Do you think I could take Goldstein?" I said. Dmitri was staring at me. Fy just sat looking down at the grass all around us.

"Is much bigger than you," Benny said.

"That's not an answer to my question."

"We kick your ass at football every time," Benny said.

"He means no," Dmitri said. "You don't take Goldstein. Why would you try?"

"Because he's a shithead."

"Trying to fight him might help," Dmitri said. "But probably won't. And you get beat up."

"What if I didn't," I said.

"You would," Dmitri said.

"Why don't you talk to Yelizaveta?" Fy said.

"She won't beat you up," Benny said.

Fy laughed. I looked at him. He just put his eyes back to the grass.

"I have talked to her," I said. "She's not my problem. My problem is that asshole."

"Is it?" Dmitri said.

"He is asshole," Benny said. "Is true." He tore some grass up. He pulled it all into his fist. Then he threw it down beside him. Dmitri stared at him now.

"What?" Benny said. "He is asshole."

"You're right," Dmitri said. "We can fight him. Samuel doesn't."

"Why's that?" I said. "We see him in gym every day. I'll go after him there."

"Is very stupid," Dmitri said.

"Why?" I said.

"Because you can't take him," Dmitri said. I wanted each of them to be every bit as angry at Goldstein as I was. I wanted every person in all of Pikesville—in all of Baltimore—to want to see Goldstein get beat up as badly as I did.

"Fine. So maybe it doesn't happen at school then," I said. "Maybe I'll see him at a party sometime. And then I'll kick his ass."

"You can't kick ass," Benny said.

When we got to the kitchen we found Mrs. Zilber sitting at the dining room table. But instead of the

sound of the TV droning histrionic talk show hosts we
heard the toothy vibration of Russian. In the other two
chairs at the kitchen table sat a kid about our age and a
middle-aged Russian woman. They'd not yet taken off
their coats. Dmitri's mother said something to the kid.
But before he had a chance to react, Benny held his arms
to their full wingspan, as if he were measuring the biggest
fish he'd ever caught.

"Sasha Anasha!" Benny said.

The two women looked at each other. Dmitri's mother
clicked her tongue. Benny saw them looking at each
other and said something. Again they just shrugged.
Dmitri's mother looked away. The kid at the kitchen
table stood, his face betraying no emotion. He was an
inch or two shorter than Benny. Benny walked over to
the boy and held him by the shoulders, the habitual
action of a much older man. Then he embraced him and
cradled the kid's head against his own.

"Benyachik," the kid said. The kid said something to
Benny. He said the same thing to Fy and gave him a
hug as well. Then he turned to Dmitri.

"Mitya Abramovitch," Sasha said. Dmitri didn't have
quite the same reaction that Benny had to Sasha, though
you could tell he was surprised to see him. He took the
kid's right hand and shook it while pulling the boy to him.

"Alexander Slobodsky," Dmitri said.

Then the two of them let go. The kid looked at me. He furrowed his brow.

"This is very good friend of mine," Dmitri said. "He is Samuel Gerson. Samuel, this is cousin Alexander Dmitrovitch."

"Call me Sasha, yo," the kid said.

He put out his hand to me and as he did so he thrust his shoulders back and his chest out as if the Nike swoosh embroidered on his track jacket was a military insignia he wished me to inspect. The jacket was zipped to the middle of his sternum and while initially it appeared he was wearing nothing under it but an unruly tangle of gold chains, when he shifted his position to grab my hand I could see that he wore a wife-beater underneath. A smattering of wiry chest hairs poked out amidst the gold chains. His bulbous nose was marred by acne and his chubby cheeks much the same. He said something to Dmitri.

"He is OK," Dmitri said. "Friend from gym class." Slobodsky or Sasha or whatever his name was suddenly had a crease in his brow. "And this is Aunt Lyuba," Dmitri said. The woman at the table with Mrs. Zilber stood. She didn't offer her hand. She was even more youthful than Dmitri's mother. While her son wore a tracksuit that wasn't warm enough for the weather, she wore a long white quilted coat. Her hair was bleached a blonde so platinum it was colorless. She wore a pair of off-white leather pants. Underneath Aunt Lyuba's white jacket was a tufted camel-hair sweater and strands of the light hairs drifted upward, attracted to her pale thin face, which sparkled like it had been dusted by the sand of some precious gem. All this white against her pale skin made it seem as if she was some sybaritic snow creature.

I walked to the far side of the kitchen, opposite the table where these two ethereal women fell back into conversation. I collected the Gatorades I'd brought. In the basement Benny and Sasha were already deep in conversation. As soon as Sasha saw I'd entered the room, he stopped talking. Then he and Benny started talking again. Dmitri and I sat down in the corner and turned on the Atari. We were a couple of minutes into a game of *Space Invaders* when the conversation behind us stopped.

"Yo, Atari!" Sasha said. "That shit is mad old!"

Dmitri paused the game. We both turned to look at him.

"Is game system we have," Dmitri said.

"It's cool," Sasha said. "I'm just sayin' it's mad old."

"You think we are happier if we do something else?" Dmitri said.

"Ease up," Sasha said. "But yeah—we might at least roll a blunt if we're gonna hang out. I got some Phillies, but no pot. Any of you got any?"

Sasha's affected speech was toning down, and his Russian accent, though far less pronounced than his cousin's, began to come through. Benny and Fy agreed it was a good idea to get high, but neither of them had any. They looked at me.

"I don't have any on me," I said.

"Well you need to get some then," Sasha said. He turned to me. "I don't got any on me—you down to smoke? If you got cash, I get you a bag."

"Yeah, I'm cool," I said.

"I'll hook it up," Sasha said. "I know people." As he said it his chubby cheeks went ruddy again. His eyes darted from Benny's for the first time. Dmitri didn't like his cousin's braggadocio. But he didn't like seeing him embarrassed either.

"My mother tells you moved," Dmitri said.

"Yeah," Sasha said. "We got a nice apartment down on Oceanview Avenue and Brighton Beach Thirteenth."

We turned back to the video game, and the whole time we played Benny and Sasha sat behind us talking. Though I couldn't understand what they were saying, whenever it was Dmitri's turn to play I would try to listen. Sasha told stories and Benny heeded him in a way I'd never seen him pay heed to anyone. It became clear Benny was much closer to Sasha than Dmitri was. I got the sense that if Sasha wanted Benny to do

something, Benny would do it. I'd become so distracted
by Sasha that when our game was over, Dmitri had
beaten me worse than he'd ever beaten me before.

\*

By the time night fell we had a plan: we would all go
home and at nine o'clock I was to pick Dmitri up from
his house and we'd head up Reisterstown Road to meet
Sasha. When I got to the Zilbers' house Dmitri was waiting
for me. He didn't get into the shotgun seat. Instead he
came around to my door.

"You get out," he said.

"Why?" I said.

"If you do drugs, you don't drive," he said. "I'll be
driver."

Dmitri pulled out of his development and drove up
Reisterstown Road. It was the first time he'd driven my
car. All the way he took turns too hard. He started braking
too late before we reached a red light or a stop sign and
had to stop so suddenly we both smashed forward against
our seatbelts. We rode a couple miles until the strip malls
gave way to a short stretch of industrial buildings. We
got a good ways up Reisterstown Road. There were a
number of factories out in the part of Owings Mills
we'd reached, many of which housed companies that
developed the formulas for artificial scents and flavors

that went into air-fresheners and candy. There was a particular section of the road where for a week you might smell a sharp cinnamon smell, or that artificial grape flavor that wasn't at all like the smell of actual grapes. Dmitri slowed the car when we reached the middle of those factories. He turned into a parking lot and stopped in front of a warehouse just down the road from the Owings Mills Mall. Dmitri turned off the car. The whole place was enveloped by a miasma of cherry smell.

"Liza is hooking up with Goldstein again," Dmitri said.

"I found out as a rumor. Then I asked her about it, and it's true."

"Fuckhead."

"That's what you were fighting with him about in the fall."

For a minute we both just looked out our windows.

"Sasha's a dealer," I said.

"He knows people who can get pot. It has to come from somewhere. Does cousin Sasha have power? No. But who knows? Even runt of litter sometimes grows sharp teeth. My family, we leave Russia to leave behind what Sasha wants to do now. My cousin comes to Brighton Beach and gives himself silly name, like old gangsters in Ukraine. Anasha means hashish."

"Sounds stupid."

"Of course. It doesn't make it safe to be with boy with stupid name. Is saying that says: 'Farther you stay from the Tsar, longer you live.'"

"So why did you come here tonight?"

"I don't let you come here alone, just like I don't let my friends go alone to West Baltimore. My friends might make bad decision, but when they make bad decision, I go and help them." He stopped talking. The cherry smell saturated the car. I put my hand to my nose to try to stop it, but my hand smelled of it too. I sneezed three times.

"Nazdravie," Dmitri said.

A pair of headlights lit everything in my car and now I could see Dmitri's face more clearly than ever. His haircut was much better now, neatly trimmed across his forehead. There wasn't quite as much acne as he'd had even just back in the fall. His cheeks had thinned. He'd grown older in those months since we'd met. But even in his having matured he was still so far from being a man—I realized then that I'd frequently thought of him as one. Dmitri was looking at me too. His gaze passed across my face in those few seconds that the headlights drew everything completely clear, and for those seconds it was as if we made perfect sense: Dmitri and I, here together. For the first time since we'd known each other, I realized Dmitri was scrutinizing me too. He was searching out the truth of what I was as much as I was him.

Then the beams fell away. We were covered in the smell of ersatz cherries. The car pulled up next to us. Instead of Benny's beat up old Subaru, a new, hunter green

Mitsubishi 3000GT parked next to my window. It was
the most desirable sports car that year; the only kid
who had one at Pikesville High was the son of a pitcher
for the Orioles, and his was red. This car's windows
were tinted. It sat next to us, its engine rumbling, while
I stared into that dark tinted window. I was about to
say maybe we should go when the window went down
to reveal a guy I'd never seen before. His hairline was
receding and he had an unlit cigarette dangling from
his mouth. Behind the wheel was another guy around
the same age—he had wispy blonde hair and wore a
red-and-black leather jacket with a snap across the neck,
like the one Michael Jackson wore in the video for
"Thriller" ten years earlier.

"Sorry," I said. "I think we're looking for the wrong—"

Just then Sasha poked his head up from the back seat.
"We got the bag," he said. I leaned forward and I could see
now that Benny was sitting in the back seat, driver's side.

"Get the fuck out and give him the shit," the driver
said. I got out of the car. The 3000GT was parked very
close to my Volvo, so I had to be careful not to hit its
door. The guy sitting shotgun opened his door and let
Sasha out. Dmitri got out of my car, left it running, and
came to stand next to me.

"I got the shit," Sasha said. "It's sixty an eighth."

That was generally what I paid for the best pot I
could get.

"You wanna hop in?" I said.

"No need, yo. They got the bag. Just gimme the money."

"Let's see it."

Sasha turned around. The blonde guy in the Thriller jacket said, "I thought Sasha said he was the best at slinging bags. Guess we'll have to start calling him something else. Sasha-Can't-Sell-Shit." The two older guys in the 3000GT both laughed mirthless laughs. Benny had shifted over in the backseat. He was laughing, too. I started to laugh but the guy said:

"What the fuck are you laughing about."

"Who are these kids again?" the guy in the Michael Jackson jacket said.

Sasha turned to them and said, "It's my cousin and his friend. I told you, yo—shit be aight." Then he turned back to us and said, "Fuck this! I don't know about your white-ass Baltimore way of buying a bag, but here's the Brighton Beach way: you give me money and then you get a bag."

"And then we're gonna go meet up at Dmitri's to smoke a blunt," I said.

"We got some shit to do," Sasha said. Benny just looked straight ahead. The guys in the front seat were doing the same. I took three twenties from my wallet and handed them to Sasha. He turned to the receding-hair guy, who opened the glove box. He pulled out a Ziploc bag and handed it to Sasha, who gave it to me.

"Later," Sasha said. He went to get back in the car but Benny was sitting in his seat now. "Get the fuck over," Sasha said. All three of the guys in the car laughed. Benny pushed him back, then moved over.

"Sasha Anasha," the blonde guy said. "Learning to stand up for himself, the little fuck." Now the driver put his sports car into first, circled around us and drove away. While Dmitri drove back down Reisterstown Road I unrolled the bag. It was filled with the brownest pot I'd ever seen—there were big, olive-green seeds all through-out the dry buds. They'd been pressed and bricked so that it looked like they'd been freeze-dried. I tried to get a whiff, but the only thing I could smell was the artificial cherries.

"How is this?" Dmitri said.

"The truth? Worst I've ever seen."

"I told you my cousin is not so much of gangster."

We drove back up Reisterstown Road and back to the Zilbers' house. We played Space Invaders until midnight. We were just finishing what figured to be our last game when Sasha and Benny finally showed up. Their eyes were bloodshot and they smelled like Phillies blunts.

"Look who it is!" Sasha said. "Cousin Dmitri and his boy, still playing their old ass game." Sasha looked at me. "You roll up some of that dope yet, white boy?"

"No," I said. "Dmitri doesn't smoke. I wasn't gonna smoke alone."

"Well now you got boys here," Sasha said. He put up his hand. I flinched a little. "We cool," Sasha said. He took my forearm in one of his hands and slapped me five with the other. He did that thing where you hold onto the other guy's fingers and make them snap together. "Word. I was just fucking with you before. Now let's smoke down."

I went to take out my bag and break some of the crumbling buds up. Benny looked down at the shwag on the table.

"Why don't we roll some of ours?" Benny said.

He and Dmitri were both looking at Sasha now.

"What, you not happy with your bag, homeboy?" Sasha said. We were all looking at the seeds and stems and brown buds on the table.

"You know is bad deal," Dmitri said. "Even I know it is."

At first it looked like Sasha was going to give me a hard time again. I was ready for it. But then he looked at his cousin, and back at Benny, and he pulled a bag out of his pocket.

"Oк, Oк," Sasha said. "Check it. Let's just puff down all this shit." So I rolled half of the disgusting eighth Sasha had sold me into a joint, and Sasha pulled out some huge, green buds from his bag. They were covered in little white crystals and veined with red hairs. He rolled them into a blunt. We smoked and smoked for the next hour.

"You will be OK to drive?" Dmitri said when I got ready to leave. He looked at me for a second and then he let it drop. He walked me to the front door.

"So I'll see you Tuesday," I said. He said he had plans then. "OK," I said. "Wednesday?"

"We go to Ferdyshchenko's Wednesday. You come with us. We hang out."

So I said I'd come, of course I'd come, I'd love to, there's nothing I'd like better, and I meant it.

# EIGHT

The next Sunday Yelizaveta and I went on a drive. Liza's teacher had told her that she had written so nearly great a paper on *The Great Gatsby* that she should work on some other aspect of the book for her final assignment. Apparently Yelizaveta had failed or nearly failed every other paper she'd turned in.

I was on my way out the door to pick her up when my grandfather called. I had just returned home from school and the phone was ringing. I expected it to stop, but it just kept ringing—six, seven, eight, nine rings— so I answered. There was a brief silence on the phone. I heard voices in the background. My grandfather said, "István?"

"No, it's Samuel," I said.

"Mother's papers, Sammycom," he said. "They have mother's papers, the letters, Samuel my papers! Not mother's papers!" He was breathing rapidly and gasping. In the background was some quiet, studied commotion.

I heard a woman's voice say, "Almost an hour now."
My parents had hired a nurse to look after him a
couple days a week. It must have been her talking.

"Grandpa, it's OK, just calm down. Now tell me who.
It'll be OK. Who is trying to take Grandma's papers? Is
it the nurse who's staying with you?"

"Mother's papers, Steviecom." His voice had cranked
all the way up when he first started talking. Now it wound
down. He let out a desperate sigh. "Please, please, won't
lets them takes mother's papers."

"Grandpa, tell me who is trying to hurt you. What
papers?"

"Don't!" my grandfather said. "No! Don't let! Go, run,
Samuelcom! Darling!" That part he said so loudly they
must have been able to hear it. Then his voice dropped
down: "Please, please Samuel, please don't let them take
the papers." He was weeping. It went on like this for
another couple minutes, me asking the same questions
and him gasping, until finally, after trying to talk to
him and getting only the same answers, I had to hang
up. I called my father at work.

"So that's it?" my father said.

"Yeah. Sounded bad. Like he was out of breath. What
do you think?"

"I think he's losing it," my father said. "I think he's
been losing it a long time. He's always been so burdened

by his war experiences, and Grandma. He got out, you know, but his parents and everyone else didn't."

I took off for the Zilbers'. When I picked Liza up we didn't kiss hello. We drove out through a long stretch of Dulaney Valley Road into Towson.

"So you help me write paper?" she said.

"You write it, and I'll edit. What do you want it to be about?"

"Maybe I writes about Zelda, wife."

"She was crazy, you know. She always made Fitzgerald feel like he wasn't good enough for her. They lived right out here. That's it. This is what you're going to write your paper on. I'm going to show you."

Yelizaveta turned the music up. I explained, loudly, that I was going to drive the two of us out to the St. Joseph's Medical Center.

"This is hospital?"

"It is," I said. The last time I'd been to St. Joseph's my father had taken me there to get x-rayed after a line drive broke two bones in my right arm during a game at the Towson State University campus, right next to the hospital. While we waited for my results my father told me there used to be a mansion called La Paix on that same spot. "It's where F. Scott Fitzgerald lived," my father said. "They tore it down in the '60s when St. Joseph's expanded. TS Eliot lived there in the 1930s." In the four weeks that followed he devised a small tour of literary Baltimore. We looked at pictures of the bucolic grounds of La Paix. It had long, slow porches perfectly suited for Daisy and Tom Buchanan to sit and drink. The area where the huge hospital complex now sprawled had once been acres of verdant lawn. My father took me by all the places where HL Mencken once lived and the *Baltimore Sun* offices where he'd worked and the bars where he drank. We drove by Broadway and Fayette where Edgar Allen Poe died at the old Church Home Hospital after he was found delirious and drunken, wandering the Baltimore streets.

Now I would take Yelizaveta to see La Paix myself. "So this is where it was, Fitzgerald's La Paix," I said. We drove among the dozen or so buildings that made up the hospital complex.

"Which is Fitzgerald house?" Yelizaveta said. We went past the cancer center and the outpatient building, the trauma ward and the infectious disease building, and when I got my bearings I remembered my father had driven me to the hospital power plant. It was a big square building with green aluminum siding.

"Well," I said. "There's the spot, anyway." A few old elms next to the building shook in the wind, puffed like spooked cats.

"But is just power garage," she said.

"The mansion doesn't exist anymore. Now it's just the hospital power plant."

"Is just building. Is board?" She made a square with her fingers. "Is board, I say? You know, with metal, letters, for remembering."

"Oh!" I said. "Like a plaque? Oh. Well, no."

"I wanted to see board."

"I guess it just didn't seem important enough when it was torn down for someone to put one up."

"I wanted it. You take me all way out to hospital and is nothing."

"Well, I wouldn't say there was nothing. That was where Fitzgerald and Zelda lived. You can still write about it. There just isn't anything official to commemorate it. It actually makes it more solemn, I think, don't you? To have nothing there?"

I drove for another minute before I said, "I wanted to be with you." I'd tried the entire first half of the afternoon to ignore my anger at Yelizaveta for the Goldstein stuff. But I couldn't stop. "But that didn't happen either, did it? Because of Goldstein." Yelizaveta just looked out the window. "Well, Zelda underwent all kinds of treatments for her psychological condition at Shepard-Pratt, you know," I said. "It's right here—we could go visit." Yelizaveta still just stared out the window.

"Lots of people still go there," I said. "To Shepard-Pratt. And you know she went to Johns Hopkins for treatment, too. That's where Goldstein's father works."

We rode the rest of the way back to Pikesville in silence. It became clear Yelizaveta wasn't going to be the one to break it.

"You want to stop by TCBY?" I said.

I went into TCBY. I bought us parfaits in tall plastic cups. Then I drove Yelizaveta back to her house.

"Should we go home and get started writing your paper?" I said.

"I go home for dinner," Yelizaveta said. I reached over and put my hand on her thigh, but she moved it off. I tried to kiss her. She gave me her cheek. She opened her door. Then she stabbed her long-handled plastic spoon into the melting cup of frozen yogurt, leaving it behind for me to throw away.

\*

The next day in gym class Stephanopoulos was on a rampage. Who knew what made his moods shift so violently? It was already getting a bit humid outside and in the gym it felt tropical. No one much wanted to be running around playing floor hockey—we were all about as sweaty as we could possibly get a couple minutes into the period. Dmitri and I were on a team of five. Steph pitted us against a team that included Steinbart and Goldstein. We were overmatched.

"Get on your horse there, Gerson! None of this lollygagging! Man up." My hands were on my knees. "What, you need a blow?" Steph wanted to know if I needed a rest, but Goldstein took his chance:

"Yeah, from his girlfriend Dmitri," he said.

"Fuck you," I said.

"I'm good, man," Goldstein said. "Wouldn't want to make your girlfriend Dmitri jealous."

"You better fucking watch what you say," I said. Goldstein was across the floor from me when we started yelling, but now he was walking closer. My hands were at my sides, and it felt like they were buzzing. I'd never threatened anyone before. Goldstein held his plastic hockey stick perpendicular down below his waist. I could see his hands flexing against the stick. Some kid on our team dropped the puck, but Goldstein and I just stood there looking at each other. The puck came towards us and rolled to the back of Goldstein's ankle. He turned around and when he pulled back and swung his stick I thought it was for me—I put my hands up, but he just slapped the puck away.

When the game was over I headed back to the locker room with Dmitri. There were still a couple of games going out on the court. Stephanopoulos stayed up in the gym until everyone was done playing. It would be five minutes before he came back down. Dmitri started undressing. I didn't. I walked over and stood by the showers. When Goldstein came down to the locker room, I was waiting. The center of my chest and up into my throat keep shivering like when you have the flu. But my anger kept pushing that feeling back down. Goldstein saw me standing there and I threw my shoulder into him and he slammed up against the lockers—he deflected the one good shot I had at his face and pushed me back against the tiled wall.

"C'mon, Gerson, you little pussy, give it up," Goldstein said. "You got nothing." I ran at him again and he pushed me and my feet got tangled up and I fell against a row of lockers. The couple of kids who were down there were standing behind us now. I heard them snicker. I got back up. All that anger was coursing through my veins. I swung again, and this time Goldstein just grabbed my fist. We stood that way for a second, him holding onto my hand and me trying to take it back.

"Look at this pussy," Steinbart said. He was standing right behind Goldstein.

"You're gonna hook up with my girlfriend and you won't fight me?" I yelled.

"Who would fight over that slut?" Goldstein said. "I don't care about her, Gerson. What's your deal? You used to be cool." I kept trying to pull my hand away, but Goldstein wouldn't let go. I tried to grab his shirt with my other hand, but he caught it and held it by the wrist. I was struggling to get out of his grasp. His eyes were searching mine, but I looked away. "I mean, what side are you on, anyway?" Goldstein said. "You're not one of those kids, man. You're not on that side."

"There is no side," Dmitri said. I hadn't even seen him come over. He was standing behind me. "You talk about my sister, you see what happens."

"Fuck you, Dmitri," Goldstein said.

Dmitri made a move behind me, I could feel him coming past my side, and just as he did we saw the first couple kids from the rest of our gym class coming down the stairs. Behind them was Stephanopoulos. He surveyed the scene—me and Dmitri on one side, Goldstein and Steinbart on the other, again, all our classmates surrounding us—and knew exactly what was going on.

"What's the problem here boys?" Stephanopoulos said. "Let's get undressed and back to class." I stood for a moment. I wasn't headed back to change.

"What's the issue Gerson?" Steph said. "If I don't see you moving for your locker in the next three seconds, you're going to find yourself on the way to Mr. Broz."

So Dmitri and I went back to our lockers, and Goldstein and Steinbart went back to theirs. On my way out of the locker room Steph was waiting. I expected him to yell at Dmitri, but this time he grabbed me by the arm and let Dmitri by.

"You got something you need to say to me?" he said.

"Like what," I said. I didn't drop my gaze. I looked him right in the eyes. It seemed like he might be ready to send me to Mr. Broz.

"I want five laps at the beginning of class tomorrow," he said. "Get out of here."

When I got home that evening, my family sat down for dinner together. My father was home a bit early from work. My mother asked me how my day was, and what could I tell her. I said, "So what do you think's going on with Grandpa?"

"I really don't know, Sam," my father said. "It's not good, whatever it is."

"Well did you call?"

"I called the nurse."

"And?"

"She said she was cleaning your grandfather's room like we paid her to, and she was putting away some old letters and he just flipped out," my father said.

"That's it?"

"That's it," my father said. "I'm going to take off work at the end of the week and head up to Long Island. I can't go tomorrow, Sam. I'll go the next day. We'll just have to see what it's about."

*

Next day at gym I was out running the five laps I owed Steph when a kid who wasn't in our class came out to the field. He spoke quietly to Steph off to the side of the field. I expected Steph to yell something derogatory at me again when instead he said, "Gerson, pack it in! You've got a message at the office."

Dmitri looked off at me. I just pushed my shoulders up to my ears. Both of my parents were waiting at the dining room table when I got home twenty minutes later. They both looked up at me.

"What's the deal?" I said.

"Sam," my father said. "Sam, Grandpa's dead."

"He's what?"

"Grandpa's dead. We need to go up to New York."

My mother didn't say anything. She just had her hand on my father's shoulder.

"Well, how'd he die?"

"He. Uh. Well. He killed himself. Early this morning. I tried calling there this morning but there was no answer. I called the nurse. She, uh, she found him."

"What'd he do?"

"I think that's probably enough, Sam," my mother said.

"You sure you want to know?" my father said.

"Yeah, I do."

"He slit his wrists."

So we would go to Wantagh to bury my grandfather.

*

When we reached Wantagh it was close to dusk. The
nurse had left a key under the mat. My grandparents'
house was a shabby, single-level, single-family Cape on
a long street lined with shabby, single-level, single-family
Capes. They had emigrated in 1956, having survived
the war and escaped from Hungary's Communist
government and now they were both gone.

The dim living room was lousy with Eastern European
tchotchkes, and my eyes were open to it in its parts. Jewelry
boxes with jade elephants on top, minute silver-handled
brooms and silver-plated dustpans, countless framed
pictures, and baubles of every kind sat on every surface.
Along a far wall stood a collection of *National Geographics*
my grandfather had been saving since the day he and
my grandmother and my father immigrated. Ancient
scrapbooks with cracking yellow pages and sepia
daguerreotypes stood in piles waist-high. On the big
coffee table in front of the television there was an
oxidized brass boar's head the size of a football, its
fanged mouth opened wide, and inside that mouth
the razor-sharp slot of a cigar cutter.

We all walked up to the attic. There was an empty
bedroom downstairs in the house, but not one of us
was going to sleep in it. Up in the attic the ceiling
sagged. On the walls hung black-and-white socialist
realism prints of hulking Magyar workers. Straight-

faced men and women with biceps like watermelons and thighs huge like those of superheroes carried scythes and reapers, pulling boxy hay carts. They seemed to say: Work! Serious work is the only answer to all life's problems. They were dully sketched by no more than eight or ten pregnant, heavy lines for every shape, and were in black underclothes. There were four of these woodcut prints on each wall. Before my parents walked back downstairs I said to my father, "OK if I make a call?"

"Just keep it short," he said. Both of my parents left the attic. I expected Dmitri, but got Yelizaveta.

"Oh, hey," I said. "Is Dmitri home?"

"No. He is at Ferdyshchenko."

"Oh, right," I said. I was meant to meet up with Dmitri and Benny that evening. They must have been wondering where I was.

"You see later?"

"No, no I can't. I'm in New York."

She said OK and hung up before I could say anything more. Those socialist realist paintings looked down at me in their stark black and stark white. They implored me to sit up straight. To act right. To do hard work. Toil! they said. Toil and know that the product of your work will be wheat that would grow up out of the black fields. But what work? My hands were idle. That doesn't matter! those figures wanted to tell me. Work! That's the right response to tragedy, pain and joy alike. Be a man. Leave a message. Go to a funeral. Do your work. Respond to work with more work, death with more death, anger with more anger, and know that's the way the world works.

Welcome to the world.

\*

Back out in the living room my father had set up the boxes we were going to pack. He already had many of them filled with the tchotchkes that had just an hour before been on the surfaces of that room. Without all those baubles covering the tables in the living room the place was cavernous and ranker from the smell of half a century of cigarette smoke. My father said, "Don't go into Grandpa's bedroom, Oĸ?"

"Did you?"

"Yeah. Just don't go in." I didn't ask why not. I thought I knew why not. What did a slit wrist look like? Or a bloody room? I said I wouldn't go in there.

"Do you want to help me get some of this stuff cleaned up?" he said. I'd never seen him like this. He was buzzing. He wasn't happy or energetic—but he was just moving a bit too fast. He was busy at work. Work! Here was a respite for idle hands. I would help. I would work. We went around the room wrapping the remaining sculptures in newspaper and packing boxes. My mother had gone out to buy some groceries. So my father and I filled dozens of boxes and dozens of trash bags with the refuse of my grandparents' lives. My grandmother's marzipan, carton after carton of Kool cigarettes. I scrubbed at the floors in the kitchen. My father scrubbed at the grime in the bathroom.

"Give me a hand down here," my father said. He'd forgotten having warned me off of going in there. We were working now. My grandfather's bedding had been stripped. The mattress was covered in small stains like specimens on slides. There weren't any blood traces. Maybe he'd done it in the bathtub.

My father pulled the photographs down off the walls. My grandfather's young face crossed the room and then went silently into a box. We covered all those pictures from my grandparents' bedroom in some yellowing newspaper we found in my grandfather's office. We threw them into a big cardboard packing box from U-Haul. I got on one end and my father got on the other. We hauled it to the garage.

Back in the living room we scanned what was left. We'd already packed most of it. The table at the middle of the living room was covered by a strange map, land masses described by odd geometric borders that might have been Soviet states or Hungarian counties, and it took me a moment to realize that this was only the sun-bleached pattern left around the darker spots where all the tchotchkes once sat: boundaries drawn by light and time. They'd sat so long in the same places they'd left behind an indelible print.

"If you want any of this stuff..." my father said.

I was standing next to a table on which sat only one thing: the bronze, cigar-cutting, gape-jawed boar I'd always loved but which my parents had deemed too dangerous to play with.

"Even this?" I said.

"Just be careful."

As we neared the end of packing up the living room, my father left the house. He didn't say where he was going. I had been reluctant to help with the bathroom, but with my father off unannounced I went at it with Comet. There was a green ring around the toilet water when I started, but by the time I finished you wouldn't have thought twice about filling a fishbowl with that water.

When my father returned he had a six-pack of Yuengling bottles.

"Help me with these?" he said. He'd never offered me a beer before.

"Lemme finish the toilet."

"We'll do it in the morning."

We sat and drank the beer. I had two and he drank the other four. When we got through them, my father found three more ancient Heinekens in the fridge. He had two and I had the other. Somehow this was work, too. We reminisced about the good things we remembered from when I was a kid, about ballgames and summer trips when we'd hiked in the Appalachian Mountains.

"You drink a lot with your friends?"

"Sure."

"You ever do more than drink?"

"Like what? Pot?"

"Yeah."

"Nope."

"You studying a lot?"

"Enough to get by."

I took a long tug at my beer. He gave me a hard look. Then he smiled, as if to say he was happier challenged than humored. He took an equally big gulp off his own beer.

"You got a baseball in your car?" he said.

I stepped over a half-dozen empties to get out to the driveway. I had only one glove in the way back of my station wagon. My dad wore it. I threw him soft rollers across my grandparents' empty floor. It was very serious at first, but five minutes in my father's mood grew manic again. He made funny throwing motions like a second baseman in old '30s herky-jerky films. I kept rolling grounders and he kept backing up. Finally he was all the way down the hallway, all the way to the curio with all the cartons of Kools.

"Harder," my dad said. "I never got to play ball in here when they were alive."

"What if I don't want to play in here?"

"Just throw the damn ball."

I threw him a grounder. He bobbled it, but he hauled it in. He threw it back harder than he should have. It got past me and hit the wall.

"I don't get to play baseball anymore either, you know," I said.

"Is that tough?"

"I didn't care at first. But knowing that shitheads like Jeremy Goldstein get to play and I'm out now."

"Isaac Goldstein's kid? The one from the little league team? I thought you used to be friends."

"Used to be is right. Now that kid just needs his ass kicked."

"He was always a cocky one. But let's not get ahead of ourselves. What'd he do?"

"Guy can't keep his dick in his pants."

"Oh," my father said. "I didn't know you guys were, you know, taking your dicks out of your pants." I just looked at him. "Well, OK. Yeah, that's tough stuff. Well, you're kids. That stuff passes."

"Whatever. Here comes one more."

I let go of a hard grounder. I threw it so hard I felt a little sparkle of catharsis run through my shoulder to my elbow and into my fingers. My father had always had wooden hands. The grounder skipped right off of his glove and through the glass door of the curio case. It gave a tinkle as it passed. There was a perfect baseball-shaped hole in the door. We froze. He was going to be really angry. He made his angriest, most squint-eyed face and said, "You're groundered." It was a terrible joke, but neither of us could hold our laughter in any longer.

"Never did like that old glass thing anyway," my father said. He said it through tears of laughter that filled his eyes just as they did mine until we could hardly see the empty place where he'd grown up. Then he stopped. He looked around. We looked at the clock on the wall. It was two forty-five.

"We should get some sleep," he said. He walked up to the attic. He stopped at the top of the stairs to turn around and surveyed the place. There was broken glass in front of the curio. Dust bunnies scuttled across the floorboards. Otherwise the room was almost entirely packed.

"It's always been a fixer-upper, from the day they moved in," he said. "Let the next owners deal with it."

*

The next morning we put on our good clothes and made for the Woodlawn Cemetery. Springtime was well into its thaw. A hole had been dug and little heads of grass sprouted from the brown ground. A half-dozen of my grandparents' Hungarian friends came and kissed us on our cheeks and expressed their condolences. Most of my grandparents' friends were already dead. The graveyard was acres wide and its grounds were well-kept, headstones all polished, shiny and tall. Some had golden gilt etching; all of them were evenly spaced, meticulously planned, in rows like patches of detached lower jaws.

My mother's heels made deep impressions in the soil leading to my grandfather's plot, leaving a line of holes as if for a garden row. There was a hole in the ground and a pile of fresh dun-colored dirt at its foot. Oblong rocks stuck out of it at points. Worms stretched in it like slick pink veins. My grandfather's casket was lowered down into the ground. A rabbi said Kaddish over his grave. He would have a marker now, a headstone sitting atop his bodily remains—his burial, his getting to live out his life, had given him this tangible reward. When the rabbi was done we each took a handful of dirt and threw it onto the casket. It was black and shiny like the lid of a grand piano.

We drove back to the house after the service. My father said, "Let's get the cleaning finished so you guys can get out of here." I went into the room across from my grandparents' bedroom and changed out of my suit. We all went to separate rooms in Grandpa's empty house. My mother ran out for an hour or so. Then we got together for an early dinner. My mother had brought back some Kentucky Fried Chicken.

"It was the best I could find," my mother said. She knew I hated KFC.

"It's OK," I said.

My parents each ate a couple of biscuits and a couple of chicken legs. Sometime toward the end of my last biscuit the phone rang. None of us had spoken in what felt like an eternity. My father got up and answered it.

"It's for you," my father said. Who could be calling me there? I went to the phone.

"Samuel!" Dmitri said. There was a rush behind him on the phone like he was talking from the inside of a conch shell. I remembered I'd given Yelizaveta the number here.

"Dmitri, hi," I said. "Listen—I'm sorry I missed you guys last night at Ferdyshchenko's. But I think Liza told you. Things are bad. My grandfather died."

"Samuel, OK, yes, I know—Samuel, I am in some trouble." It was very hard to hear him over all the background noise. "Samuel, shit, I don't know what I do," he said.

"Where are you? It sounds like you're in a hurricane."

"I am on Reisterstown Road," he said. "At payphone."

"OK. Calm down. Can you find a better phone?"

"Yes, sure. I will go to find it."

I hung up. I sat there waiting. The phone rang again and again while I ascended the stairs. It must have been on its sixth ring by the time I reached it.

"I am just about to hang up phone rings so much," Dmitri said.

"Sorry. I had to come upstairs."

"Oĸ, then you will call me back here," he said. He gave me the number. I called back. "Samuel, I'm in so much shit of trouble. We are. Fy, Benny, Sasha and Ferdyshchenko. Me." He didn't say anything for a couple seconds.

"Well, what?"

"We got Goldstein last night," he said.

"What does that mean, 'Got Goldstein?'"

"We went and hung out with Ferdyshchenko like we all plan."

"I'm sorry. I would have come, but with my grandfather and—"

"Sasha ended up staying in Baltimore. He comes to Ferdyshchenko with us. Ferdyshchenko asks why we hang out with you, and Benny says you are Oĸ now. Ferdyshchenko asks why, and Benny talks about how you don't like Goldstein like we don't like Goldstein. I tell them you went after Goldstein in gym class, he embarrass you. My cousin Sasha asks why, and Benny tells him thing with Yelizaveta. Ferdyshchenko hadn't heard any of it yet. Neither had Sasha. They got angry. I didn't say very many things. I could have. At first I said we should be calm, but they all got so angry. Then I did, too. I could have been calm, and stopped it all from happening. I could have.

"In past I would tell them even more we should keep even. We all hate asshole. We kick his ass last time he talked to Yelizaveta, so why not now? Why would we let it happen, Benny says. They do not hate you, I say, and he is with Liza, and we don't kick Samuel's ass. Samuel is Oк, Benny says.

"So we are all talking about it. Ferdyshchenko said how in same place where he lived, where we were, is where Goldstein lives."

"Wait," I said. "Ferdyshchenko lives in Arbor Estates?"

"His aunt who brings his family over to States is real estate. So Alex says he knows which one is house where Goldstein lives. I say I will drive and keep them from getting out of control, and next thing we are all in front of door together. Benny starts to pound at door. Then we see maid through peephole. I tried to say to Benny— maybe Goldstein isn't home, is just maid—but Benny takes Club and smashes window next to door."

"The Club?"

"Club. Thing to lock car steering wheel so no one steals it. Club. Benny wanted it in case Goldstein had friends over at house, so he brought it. He opened door. Maid is yelling, and she says, 'Get out of house,' but we all came inside. Goldstein was yelling from living room about, 'What is going on?' Everyone goes into house. He is there with TV. Benny says fuck you. Goldstein is standing now and maid just goes into front of house. Goldstein is stupid and he doesn't want to back down to fight when there are five of us. Goldstein say, 'You get fuck out of house, Russians.' Sasha yells something and Benny yells something and I almost yell something, too—but again Goldstein says, 'Get fuck out of house.' And then Benny smashes Goldstein's face. His face is broken, but he punches Benny hard. Benny has swollen eye, so he jumps on top of Goldstein and swings at his face again with Club. Goldstein gets hand up before it hits him in head, it hits forearm. Goldstein runs at me. He gets me by sweatshirt and pulls it so I let it go over my head like in hockey fight. What can I do but fight back? Sasha kicked Goldstein and jumped on him and hit him and punched him. Then Goldstein hit Sasha hard. So Fy hit him in face and he was bloody and down and didn't look like he gets up. We saw how bloody he was, not moving, so I say: 'We must go.' I say, 'Is pool house where Ferdyshchenko goes to smoke pot, we all go in different directions for to be safe and meet up there.' We got out of front door and all go in different direction in case anyone is seeing us and I make it to pool house. I wait and wait, but nothing. And from doorway I see it—police come. They has Fy and Benny and Alex. By now Sasha is back in Brighton Beach. I couldn't stay at home. And my sweatshirt is left behind. They'll be looking for me."

"What sweatshirt were you wearing?" I said. "The one that Goldstein pulled off you?"

"Baltimore Orioles," he said.

"That shirt has my name in it."

"Who gives fuck about sweatshirt! Or about Goldstein! I will come over to your house."

"I'm not here. I'm in New York. On Long Island. My grandfather died on Tuesday."

"Is even better," Dmitri said.

"We're not there."

"Is there way into house?"

"Not really." Now I would be truly complicit with Dmitri and his friends. This was all the way to the other side. I suppose I could have gotten out of it then, told Dmitri I wanted nothing to do with this, with him. But I was already part of a causal chain. It was already too far. I said, "Sometimes the back window is open."

"I go there."

"You could, but," I said. "Or you could—"

But Dmitri had already hung up.

# NINE

My mother and I took my parents' Volvo back to Baltimore after my grandfather's funeral. My father was to spend the next week getting my grandparents' estate in order. A heavy fog had settled over the roads of Pikesville when we got off the highway. When we turned onto our street and neared our yard, our house, and our juniper bushes, and the big old elm on the front lawn, were lit by a thin red light. Then the whole yard and the house glowed with a blue light. It changed again and again in flashes.

"Jesus Christ," my mother said. As we pulled up closer to the house, I saw what she had seen. "Police?" she said. "What on Earth?"

A Baltimore County Police car was parked in our driveway, blocked from view by our next door neighbors' mound of lawn. There was no one behind the wheel and its lights were flashing. I pulled up into the driveway, behind the police car. My mother and I got out. She speed-walked in front of me.

"What on Earth is going on at my house?" my mother said.

"Ma'am, there's just been some trouble," the police officer said.

"Trouble?"

"There's been a break-in," he said. Just then another uniformed police officer came from behind the house. I was standing at the bottom of the steps that led to our front door. The officer coming from the back looked at me.

"Nothing more back there," he said.

"What was there?" my mother said.

"Ma'am," the second officer said. "Ma'am, you been broke into."

"We just heard. Did they get the good jewelry?"

"We don't know if anything's been taken," the second officer said. "We come by and when we get here and check out back and see one of the basement windows been broken, my partner, he come around back and the kid was off running."

"Did they get him?" I said.

"Oh, we got him," the second officer said. He gave me a long hard stare. There were some cobwebs stuck onto his hair from his poking around out back.

"Well at least there's that, for heaven's sake," my mother said.

The first officer looked back at my mother.

"I wonder if you'd let my partner in so we can look to see if anything's been taken?" the first officer said. "Just a procedural inspection."

"Yes, of course," she said. My mother led the second officer into our house. She turned on the foyer light. We all stood for a moment just inside the doorway. Everyone's pupils shrank down to small black dots.

"I'd like to talk to you out front," the first officer said to me. My mother was already down the basement stairs with the second officer. I followed the first officer back out to the front steps. Now the white light of the house cast across our backs, knocking out the effect of the flashing lights that splashed over the front lawn. The fog had grown so thin it was hardly noticeable. "The kid we got from the basement was Dmitri Zilber," he said. "He was wanted in the assault of this other kid, this Goldstein kid. Do you know Dmitri Zilber?"

I told him I did.

He held his shoulders back and straight. Now his lips spread into a line across the center of his face.

"Honest," he said. "That's good. And do you know this Goldstein kid?"

"Yes."

"This Zilber kid is in some serious trouble. Breaking and entering, assault, and now a second B and E. We found him here after we came looking to talk to you—

your name was on an item of clothing found at the scene of the Goldstein assault. But the Zilber kid made clear the item was his. Is he a friend of yours?"

I said he was. Now the officer didn't say a word. A stale cambric whiff lifted off the stiff twill of his navy blue uniform. "MERKER" was etched in black print on the scuffed bronze nameplate attached to his chest. There were patches on each of his shoulders that said Baltimore County Police Department.

"Ok. I'll ask you this: Were you at this Goldstein kid's house on Wednesday night?" Officer Merker said. The line of his lips pushed back into a crumpled wave. There was a gun on his hip. His face was tied together in a tight knot.

"I was in Long Island for my grandfather's funeral. We just got back. That's where we were. Since Tuesday."

"I'm sorry," he said. I cocked my head. "About your grandfather. So have you talked to this Zilber?"

All I said was: "Yes." Then I said, "Aren't we supposed to be in some room with a two-sided mirror or something?"

"You watch too much TV," he said. "Why don't we take a seat here." We sat on the front step. "Did you know this Zilber kid was coming to your house?" he said. "This Zilber kid said he talked to you. He said you gave him permission to come to your house. So. Did you know he was coming to your house?"

"He knew he could come to my house if he needed to. We're friends."

"Oĸ," Officer Merker said. "Oĸ, I'll buy that. Another question: this detail doesn't make sense to me, the sweatshirt with your name in it at the scene."

"It was my sweatshirt."

"And now this Zilber kid had it," Officer Merker said. Some of the neighbors' lights were coming on. A couple I didn't know was standing across the street in their driveway, looking at us.

"I don't know how much of any of this I should be saying," I said.

"You've said a lot already."

"You never read me my rights."

"This Goldstein kid's already told us you weren't there. I'm sure we wouldn't even be talking to you if it wasn't for this Zilber kid being here. This isn't *LA Law*. We don't need evidence. Some kids beat some other kid up pretty bad. The beat-up kid told us all about it. We're looking for one more kid and we know it isn't you. And this stuff will disappear if those kids are adjudicated minors anyway, depending what a judge decides."

"What does that mean?" I said.

"Here's the deal," Officer Merker said. "Just out of my own curiosity. I tell you something, you tell me something. Good?" I wasn't sure if I should agree or not. "Look," he said. "Usually with these things—you kids are what, like fifteen or something?"

"I'm sixteen," I said. "Seventeen in a month. Dmitri's a year younger. Don't know his birthday. I think some of his friends might be a little older."

"So, yeah," he said. "That Goldstein kid got beat up pretty good. But he'll heal. So most likely, if they got at all good of a lawyer, they can all get their cases moved to juvenile court. The older ones maybe not, but if your friend is fifteen, he'll probably get out of adult court in a month or so."

"Then what?"

"He'll go to Hickey till he's eighteen or nineteen. This is county though, so who knows. Judge might wanna make an example."

I couldn't imagine Dmitri behaving well in a detention center. The flashing lights of the police car cast over us again. Lights came on and went off in houses across the street. The fog was settling back in.

"So now you," he said. "What's the deal?"

"The Goldstein stuff?"

"Whatever you know about."

"The sweatshirt was mine. There are a lot of clothing drives. For new kids. Dmitri—the Zilber kid—got mine."

"And you were friends?" Officer Merker said.

"That's kind of how we got to be friends."

"Huh. And that's what those kids were fighting over?"

"No. That was over a girl."

"Oh, right. That's not how this Goldstein kid is telling it, but that's what the other kids said. What girl?"

"Yelizaveta," I said.

"That's this Zilber kid's sister?"

"I think this might be my fault."

Actually, I thought I might pass out. The blue and red lights flashed. I thought I might throw up.

"But you weren't there," Officer Merker said.

"I was together with Dmitri's sister. I hated Goldstein. Me and him even got in a fight in school last week." Officer Merker seemed to be looking at my skinny arms. "It didn't go very well. Goldstein's a lot bigger than me. Mostly I was trying to get Dmitri and his friends pissed at him. I think that's why they went."

"That's not a crime."

"It's not?"

"I'm not wasting the city's time and money hauling you down to the station for it, if that's answer enough," he said. "You gotta live with it if you feel you put them in the situation, but that's on you. That's an issue you create. It's not a legal thing." The two of us sat together for what felt like a long time. Some of the neighbors' porch lights came on. Some of the lights in their windows went off. There was no sense of relief. I felt the muscles in my back tighten.

The other officer came down the steps from the second story of my house. I could hear my mother saying, "I'm just glad nothing was taken after all. What a relief!"

"Coulda been a whole lot worse, no doubt," the second officer said.

Officer Merker took out his card and handed it to my mother.

"If you find anything you thought was here is gone, just give a call," he said. "And you might look into a better alarm system." He pointed to the turn-key box on the wall next to our front door. It had a red bulb over it like on the nose to the guy in the board game *Operation*. If the front or back door opened it made a loud buzzing sound. None of our other doors were hooked up to it. It hadn't gone off when Dmitri broke our back window.

"What's this, like, 1972?" the second officer said.

"We didn't think we needed it," my mother said.

"Maybe you don't," Officer Merker said. "If you have any more questions about this, call."

"Wait," my mother said. "You said you caught whoever did this?"

"We've got him," Officer Merker said. "Someone your son knows, boy named Dmitri Zilber. Kid we won't have to worry about again. Right?"

"I guess not," I said. My mother shot me a look. When she saw my face her skepticism turned to concern.

"Most likely you can just get him to pay restitution. But if you'd like to press charges..."

"I couldn't say without talking to my husband," my mother said. "What do people usually do?"

"People in my neighborhood don't usually sue when a window been broken," the second officer said. He looked at Merker and smiled. Merker didn't.

"You've got my card," Officer Merker said.

\*

I was in my room for a good half hour before I heard my mother's footsteps.

"Just lying there," she said.

"Waiting for you to come down on me."

"Over what? You didn't tell Dmitri to break into our house."

"I told him he could come over. I knew Dmitri was in trouble and I told him he could get in through a back window."

"Since when could anyone ever get into this house through a back window?" my mom said.

"Well. Sometimes I leave it open to sneak in," I said. "But I wasn't sure if it was or if it wasn't. So I told him he could get in and hide here."

"You did." She walked up next to my bed. The skin around her eyes drew taut in a way it only did when she was about to yell. Then it went back to normal. "So you did," she said. "But you didn't tell him to break the window." And there was nothing to do then but tell her what had happened with Dmitri and his friends and Goldstein. And how I felt it was my fault because of Yelizaveta and how angry I'd been.

"This isn't you, Samuel. None of this. The worst you'd been a part of before Dmitri came around was staying up too late on the phone." I sat up. I picked up a CD case and tapped it against my knee. My mother sat down on the couch across from my bed. I was sure she would sit down on the bed next to me, like she always did, but she was across from me.

"I'm more worried about Dmitri than me right now," I said. "That officer said they'll send him to Hickey. Jesus. That's it for him."

"It would help if he had a good lawyer."

"Do we know one?"

"Dick Weintraub," my mother said.

The CD case went silent. She closed her eyes. There was a hum that sometimes came on underneath the floorboards in my room when the furnace was on. You never really noticed it when it started up, but when it shut down, it was hard not to sense something had changed in the tenor of the room. The hum had been on the whole time we were talking. Now it stopped. The room went silent.

Then, finally, my mother was just my mother again. She came over to my bed, sat down next to me, and held my face against her chest. It had been so long since I'd felt that safety, like my mother would fend off malicious advances from strangers and scare away bullies and kiss away the sting of a scraped knee and make it heal. We sat there together for a long time.

\*

I tried calling the Zilbers' house many times in the month after Dmitri's arrest. No one answered. Yelizaveta never returned my calls and she stopped coming to school. Then one day at the end of May, after having been denied bail for fear he was a flight risk, and having spent most of the month in jail in Towson, Dmitri was arraigned in front of a Circuit Court judge. Dmitri's family had accepted my mother's offer for him to be defended by Dick Weintraub. Dick called the morning Dmitri was arraigned to say he'd gotten Dmitri transferred to juvenile court where he'd be tried the next morning. He'd also called to say that Dmitri had refused his representation any longer and would be using a public defender. Benny, Alex and Fy were all going to be tried as adults. They were all seventeen; they all had state-appointed lawyers. Dmitri was the lucky one. I knew Goldstein couldn't identify Sasha, and Dmitri and his friends wouldn't tell the police his name. He'd most likely taken off for Brooklyn like Dmitri said he would, and the cops wouldn't care to track him down.

I drove to Towson the next morning. The Baltimore County Courts Building is a monolithic edifice, four stories of gray sandstone and '60s communist-block architecture. In the lobby I passed through a metal detector. Hearing Room B, where juvenile trials are held, was just around the corner. Inside, five wooden benches sat in pairs down to the front. There were maybe two-dozen people seated in them. The room had very low ceilings and fluorescent lighting that wasn't sufficient to illuminate the entire space. At the far end the judge's bench was elevated four or five feet above the floor. Two tables sat before it. Baltimore County police officers stood at attention at either side. The juveniles and their lawyers stood behind a table in front of the judge and to the right, with the State's Attorney behind a table to the left.

The day's docket was already in progress. Yelizaveta and Mrs. Zilber sat at the front of the room. I took a seat in the back. I looked at the backs of the heads of the people two rows in front of me for a minute before I recognized they belonged to Jeremy Goldstein and his parents.

As the juveniles were brought up, police officers came in and out of the courtroom to testify to arrests they'd made if the case was contested. This was the machinery, the bureaucracy witnessed only by those whose fate had been placed in someone else's hands. The State's Attorney read through the cases and the offenders' lawyers pleaded for leniency. Even so, these kids up for dispensation were as obsequious and dazed as those who were being arraigned. They all just wanted to avoid being sent to Hickey.

The docket moved forward. Not one kid we saw disputed the charges against him. They all accepted the accusations, presented a case for themselves—their grades, their remorse—and waited for the judge to tell them how long their community service or detention was to be.

The only contentious case was of a kid who'd stolen a car. The State's Attorney read through the charges: this car thief had been chased by the police for ten blocks. He had taken out mailboxes and hedgerows. The State's Attorney read a statement from a police officer who, after the thief had been detained, had overheard the kid saying: "They couldn't catch my ass! I'm gonna be a race car driver, I'm Mario-motherfucking-Andretti."

"I don't think you'll be driving for a long time, young man," the judge said.

Precarious laughter spread through the hearing room.

"I can drive good," the car thief said.

"What's that, son?" the judge said. For the first time the mood in the room shifted. Until now the judge spoke and the kids demurred. There was a sense of paternal ease to the judge. His large jowls rested uncomfortably on the neck of his black robe. The lawyers all referred to him as Master Brown—juvenile court judges were called Master Chancellor—and Master Brown had been speaking to the car thief as he did to the kids who came before him. He spoke as if he was their father, as if doling out punishment was so natural to him it was too mundane to display emotion while doing it. But now Master Brown's jowls colored.

"You took out three mailboxes and totaled a stolen car," he said. "You drive poorly. You don't drive 'good.' You won't be driving for a long, long time. And you won't walk out of here ever if you don't change your attitude." The car thief looked down at his feet. Master Brown went through the litany of questions he asked every defendant as he or she came before him:

"What's your age?" Master Brown said.

"Fifteen," the car thief said.

"Do you read and write the English language?"

"Yeah."

"Do you use drugs?"

"No."

"Do you take any prescribed medication?"

"Nope."

"Are you currently seeing a psychiatrist?"

"Yeah."

The car thief had no lawyer. Now that he understood Master Brown could be made to care about what happened in his courtroom, whatever élan had caused the kid to outrun the police and then brag about it evaporated into the stale courtroom air.

"Now you were going to plead not guilty, son," Master Brown said. "That means we have to ask this police officer to come and testify and tell us what we already know: you stole that car. You want to do that?" Everyone turned to see that a police officer sat in the row behind the car thief's mother. It was Officer Merker.

"No, sir," the car thief said.

"No sir what?"

"I can go on and plead guilty. I done what they said I done."

"Ok," Master Brown said. "Am I going to see you here again with the attitude you came in with today, young man?"

"No sir. I can do good." Master Brown looked at the kid. His anger transformed back into a mighty indifference. "Ok. Let's do it as eight weeks in Hickey. Then we'll have you here again—and you'll tell me you've given your behavior some long thought so you can go back home." Master Brown pushed his chair back. The car thief was led out of the hearing room. The State's Attorney pulled out a file from the pile of folders in front of him and looked it over.

"Case 06901," he said. "This one's the assault that's being contested. Dmitri Abramovitch Zilber." The State's Attorney couldn't have been a day older than Officer Merker. He wore a billowing beige suit one size too large and he kept touching his perfectly gelled brown hair as if there were bangs there to wipe from his eyes.

"This is the one they're transporting from Hickey?" Master Brown said. The State's Attorney whispered with another younger man off to the side, the representative from the Department of Juvenile Services.

"He's here now," the State's Attorney said. "Should we have them bring him in?"

The brown-shirted police officer from the Baltimore County Sheriff's Office went out through the door behind him. Yelizaveta turned to her mother. Mrs. Zilber just looked forward. When she turned, Liza saw me for the first time. Her nostrils flared. She turned back.

Dmitri came through the door next to Master Brown's bench. He wore a dirty white t-shirt and baggy jeans and although there wasn't far for him to walk to get behind the defendants' table, his gait was stilted. His ankles were shackled together. The shackles were just a thin chrome chain—the parts wrapped around his ankles were invisible, swallowed up by his jean legs. The brown-shirted officer clutched him mid-bicep. Dmitri's face was stolid as ever—his eyes narrowed, his mouth a pencil-drawn line. His public defender joined him at the table. Dmitri's mother and Yelizaveta stood and moved into the middle of the aisle. The State's Attorney read from the case file.

"On the evening of April 27, the respondent and three of his friends broke into the house of Jeremy Goldstein at 223 Arbor Lane, in the Arbor Estates housing development in Pikesville. They entered the house after using a weapon to break a window by the front door and gain access to the domicile. They proceeded to assault the victim with a deadly weapon. The respondent attacked the victim, then fled the scene."

"Your honor," the public defender said. "We'd like to emend this part to note that Dmitri came into contact with the victim only when provoked. The victim has confirmed this claim." The public defender was a small man about Dmitri's height. He was bald across the top, with tufts of gray hair sticking out from either side of his head. He wore a burgundy jacket and a pair of brown dress pants that looked as old as their owner. He kept his hands stuffed down into his deep pockets.

"The victim here?" Master Brown said.

Goldstein and his father stood up. Dr. Goldstein had his arm around Goldstein's shoulders, and it made Goldstein look much younger than he was—or maybe just his age, and my memory had made him into an adult, a man, for far too long. The State's Attorney agreed to the change. The prosecutor laid out the facts of the case. Now Master Brown set out his litany of questions: How old are you? Do you read and write English? Do you use drugs and alcohol? Are you taking any prescribed medication? Dmitri answered each of the questions. The ease of questioning restored the light tone that had been broken by the car thief. But when Master Brown said, "And are you currently seeing a psychiatrist?" Dmitri's attitude changed. His shoulders drew back and he stood erect.

"What kind of question do you ask?" Dmitri said. Master Brown's jowls colored again. The whole room braced for a response like the one we had just seen in response to the car thief. The juveniles and their families had seen how Master Brown treated the kids under his gaze all morning; the juveniles who awaited trial all saw how the kids before them were treated. Only Dmitri, who had been locked up, didn't understand this was just procedure.

"It's one you have to answer, son," Master Brown said.

"Of course I don't see psychiatrist! Is not necessary. Is not what I need. I feel at all times my emotions. I do not need to talk to doctor about it."

"Well I think we can safely say that's not the case," Master Brown said. He looked down at Dmitri. Dmitri stared back. Master Brown wasn't ready to take Dmitri down like the car thief, but Dmitri's inborn truculence— that dose of Mitya Karamozov's sensualism he'd proclaimed to me the previous fall, a day that suddenly felt like years before—was on display.

"So the respondent is disputing the state's case?" Master Brown said. Before Dmitri's public defender could respond, the State's Attorney explained that Dmitri refused to agree to the terms that had been set. He didn't accept his guilt in the case. He refused to pay restitution to the Goldsteins.

"So what's there to question here, Mr. Zilber?" Master Brown said. "You broke into this kid's house, right?"

"I was with friends. I am there to make sure nothing bad happens. I am always a loyal friend, and I would not let my friends go ahead for a thing like this without me there to protect them."

"Well, the victim has a broken jaw," Master Brown said. "I think that's something bad. Don't you? Doesn't seem you helped much. And what about this other kid who you haven't identified?"

"I will not tell you any names of people. I do not put my friends in trouble."

"I don't see that helping your situation much, son," Master Brown said. He looked out into the courtroom. "Could we get the victim down here?"

Goldstein held himself differently now. His goofy insouciance was gone. Only Liza and I could see the daft smirk in his eyes as he walked toward the bench. The Goldsteins stopped just behind Liza and her mother. It took Liza a minute to realize what was happening. When she did, she took her mother by the arm. She and Mrs. Zilber moved to the side. All three Goldsteins stood next to the Zilber women now.

"You were hurt pretty badly?" Master Brown said. Goldstein started to talk, but he just emitted some hostile sound of affirmation through his clenched teeth.

"My son's jaw is wired shut," Dr. Goldstein said. "He has multiple fractures to his mandible and he lost three teeth. He had a clean break to his ulna. All because of the danger these gangsters present."

Goldstein said something again when his father finished talking. It was impossible to understand his English. The change in the way he held himself was a product of the physical pain he must still have been feeling, and right then Dmitri said, "I'm not dangerous gangster! I'm not in gang! Goldstein has attacked me and my sister and at his house he attacks me. This boy goes around in his town like he is little prince, like he can do what he wants whenever and to whoever he wants. And you will reward this? As is always rewarded? I don't pay rich kid's hospital money."

"Hey!" Master Brown said. "You'll address your comments to me. This isn't *Montel Williams*. Mr. Zilber, you came to this boy's house and attacked him. I'm not sure what there is to contest. Have we gotten anywhere with figuring out who this other unnamed kid was?"

Dmitri said nothing. Dmitri's public defender took his hands from his pockets.

"Your honor," he said. "Dmitri does not have prior contacts with the system. This gang accusation is specious. Boys hang out in groups. Dmitri is a straight-A student. We have letters written by two of his teachers saying he is amongst their smartest students." The public defender submitted the letters to Master Brown. "He has no record of drug use. And he paid restitution to the residents of the Overbrook break-in."

"Are the residents from that break-in here now?" Master Brown said. Everyone in the courtroom turned. I stood. Dmitri, Yelizaveta, Goldstein, their parents—they all looked at me. I met eyes with Officer Merker. He just looked down. Liza did the same. Dmitri's demeanor didn't change when he saw me. I don't know if I was expecting him to smile. He sure didn't.

"Well?" Master Brown said.

"Dmitri paid for the window and everything," I said.

"Your parents aren't here?"

"They sent me."

"Oκ," Master Brown said. "That will be all. Thank you." I sat down. My legs were shaking. Master Brown looked at the documents before him.

"Well, you're right," Master Brown said. "He has good grades. DJs says he's been co-operative. And yes, great grades. Smart kid. But it seems maybe his being so smart is part of these anger problems. He has a history of fights at the school."

"That information is not admissible as evidence," the public defender said.

"It is for his dispensation," Master Brown said. "I think we've moved that far."

Master Brown looked at Dmitri again. He hoped having made his point—that Dmitri's pleading not guilty had been for naught—would restore Dmitri's sense. But Dmitri was so indignant I doubt it would have made much difference. The dismissal of his plea had made Dmitri's anger grow and it was as if the wraiths of his grandfather and his father, Mitya Karamazov and Rogozhin and all the sensualists who had come before him for centuries, stood behind him there.

"I don't see how we can dispute your client's guilt," Master Brown said. "Let me ask the victim. Mr. Goldstein, do you feel Mr. Zilber continues to pose a threat?"

Goldstein uttered a final susurration. He nodded and nodded.

"A threat to him?" Dmitri said. "What kind of threat am I to boy who owns whole world! Look at him still, standing there!" That was all Dmitri got in before Master Brown slammed his hand down on his bench.

"That's the end of it, Mr. Zilber. I'm going to commit you to Hickey for eighteen months. If you show you can get a handle on this behavior we can look into moving you to an outdoor education facility." Master Brown closed Dmitri's file. The brown-shirted police officer came over and took him by the arm.

"Can't I at least say goodbye to mother and sister?" Dmitri said. Master Brown looked back up. His face betrayed only a return to his endemic indifference.

"Doesn't bother me," he said. Officer Merker left through the back door. The Goldsteins followed. Dmitri went to hug Yelizaveta. He hugged his mother. I expected to see his face change as he put his head over each of their shoulders, but as he hugged them he simply looked directly ahead. His face was frozen in that same stolid stare, his eyes looking up rather than down at the floor. It was hard to trace his gaze. All I could tell was that it was fixed on some blank spot at the back of the room.

*

I waited outside of the Courts Building on Bosley Avenue for nearly an hour after Dmitri was led out of Hearing Room B, until Yelizaveta and Mrs. Zilber came out. Mrs. Zilber walked off to wait for Yelizaveta by Dmitri's Honda—it was parked illegally in front of the building. Two parking tickets were tucked under the windshield wiper.

"What'd Dmitri say?" I said.

"What will he say?" Yelizaveta said. "He goes to Hickey." Sweat trickled down my lower back. Yelizaveta fished around in her purse and pulled out a pack of Parliaments. She took one out and lit it. She didn't offer me one. Mrs. Zilber was waiting for Yelizaveta to come to the car. She was looking and not looking at us. I stepped a little closer to Yelizaveta, so that I was right beside her. She pushed me back with the heels of both of her palms.

"You not call to our house," Yelizaveta said.

"Because Dmitri doesn't want me to anymore?"

"No," she said. "Because I want you not. You think you just apologize and is good?"

"I could try."

"You try nothing! Dmitri goes to Hickey. This is fuck. Is fuck! And you are fuck, too. This world is Samuel's world like is Goldstein's world. You come to court and stand in back and say thing, and think it makes it done? Then is done. Don't call. Don't say other things, ever."

Then Liza turned around and walked to her mother. It was such a humid day it was as if some aqueous barrier was growing in the space between where I stood and the Zilbers' car. The two Zilber women put their windows down. They had no air conditioning. I could hear Mrs. Zilber put the radio up. They were listening to Madonna. Neither of them looked my way again.

Ever.

# TEN

Nothing was resolved between Tanya and me in the first summer months after Dmitri's hearing. For weeks she didn't return my calls. I called once a day, and when I didn't call, I sat around thinking about what I would say when I got her answering machine next. Sometimes I dropped by Weiss's. Tanya's parents only said hello and went back to their work. I could only imagine what they must have thought of me.

Then at the end of the first week of August, after what must have been the fiftieth message I left, Tanya called. It had been months since I'd spoken to anyone other than my parents. Her call consisted of our not acknowledging any of what had happened and her asking me to meet up at the Suburban Club, where Tanya spent summer days tanning. When I arrived that day, the parents of many of our classmates lay sunning themselves around the pool. They were all anesthetized by the sun. SPF's 10 through 30 lay discarded under lounges. Tanya was there with them, sleeping on the far side of the pool. She was wearing a pink and blue polka dot bikini. Her arm hung, listless, off her chaise lounge.

"So," she said.

"So," I said. "What've you been up to?"

"Same as always," she said. We talked, then hit a lull in our conversation. Tanya said, "Do you want anything? A drink or something? I could grab you a snack."

There was a squat cantina at the far end of the pool that sold ice cream bars and creamsicles and Maryland Crab Cake sandwiches. In summers past Tanya had given me her family's account number.

"Yeah, a Coke," I said. "But I'll go do it."

"I'd better do it," she said. "Just wait here." I laid back down. Even after Tanya returned with our drinks and a sandwich I hadn't asked for, I felt the scrutiny of all the eyes at the club on me.

"Are you OK, Sam?" Tanya said. "You're looking a little sweaty."

"It's about six-hundred percent humidity out here."

"Now Samuel, you know that there can't, by definition, be more than one hundred percent of anything."

"Listen, Tanya," I said. "I know you must think that I fucked up so big. I know I was an asshole, but—"

"Stop," she said. We were both quiet for a minute. I could smell the sweat evaporating off my burning skin.

Tanya said, "I don't think a post-mortem of the past six months is going to help anything. I love you, Sam. You're my best friend and no matter how pissed you've made me, I need you. But it's going to take a while for us to be able to talk about some stuff.

"Let's just get some sun and then play a couple sets."

We went and played tennis on the hard-tru courts off behind the pool—T. Weiss def. S. Gerson, 7-6 (13-11), 6-2, 6-0—and shook hands more politely than I'd ever shaken hands with anyone.

"You can shower in the locker room," Tanya said when we'd finished.

"I'm due home," I said. And I went.

*

We'd all known kids who'd been shipped to Hickey for various offenses during high school—for selling drugs, usually, or driving drunk too many times— and who went off for a couple of months at a time. Invariably they returned more obedient, and angrier at their forced obeisance. A number of years after we graduated from high school Hickey would be shut down by the state after a scandal involving the mistreatment of kids by the guards there. I did my best to imagine Dmitri, like his grandfather and mine, knew his way around that stuff.

I graduated from high school without hearing from Dmitri or Liza again. During my freshman year at school in Maine my parents moved down to Florida, where my father took a post at a hospital in Gainesville. I didn't return to Baltimore again except to clean out my room just before they moved. Then one day early in my sophomore year I got an email from Dmitri. It came from the email address dabramo2@yahoo.com. It said:

Out of detention. Found your email, but new to it. You around? Call, then.

There was no sign-off. When I replied the next morning asking if this was in fact Dmitri, and what he was doing, I simply received a message later that day that said:

Same place in Greenhill. Come whenever.

When I arrived at the Zilbers' I saw that their house was virtually unchanged. The screens on their outer door were a bit rustier, but the same double helix of wires twisted out of the light fixture next to the door. The same thumb-sized hole was ripped in one of the first floor window screens. Paint flaked off the gray aluminum siding. As I walked up, Dmitri was on his way out. The door opened just as I reached it, and

Dmitri was already turned around, locking up. I stood there with Dmitri's back to me and waited for him to recognize that I was standing there. Finally he turned around.

"What?" Dmitri said. He squinted at me.

"Dmitri—I emailed," I said. "To say I was coming down. But. If it's a bad time?" The tiny creases that had developed around Dmitri's purple-bagged eyes relaxed minutely. A small wave of recognition crossed his face.

"Oh," Dmitri said. "Samuel Gerson," he said. "I did not recognize you with this." Dmitri reached out and tugged on the long, curly ponytail behind my head.

"I grew it out," I said. We stood for a moment without saying anything.

"I've got to go do something," Dmitri said. "You'll come." Just then a flock of sparrows rose up out of a juniper next to Dmitri's doorway. They lifted out like opening shots of a fireworks display. Then, all at once, they dropped back into the bush like a videotape of the same shot rewound. Dmitri and I walked out to the old beater of a Buick LaSabre I'd parked behind. There was an acrid smell inside like someone had recently vomited.

Dmitri drove to Reisterstown Road. The familiar sight of strip malls giving way to industrial buildings passed before us, and it became clear we were heading back down to that same part of Owings Mills where the artificial smell factories were located. As we neared that same block where we'd met up with Dmitri's cousin years before, a thick cherry smell filled the car. Dmitri parked in the same warehouse lot where we'd met up with Sasha. He turned the car off and faced me.

"It's a couple of minutes early," Dmitri said. "We'll wait." He was silent for a minute. "So you got into college?"

"Up in Maine. This summer I'm going to travel in Europe for a while. To Budapest to visit some of my cousins."

"Must be nice," Dmitri said.

"What about you?"

"What about what?"

"Oh," I said. "How long have you been home?"

"Couple of months."

"What about Liza?"

"She's off to community college, Catonsville. But later. I have to go in here," Dmitri said. He looked at his watch. "You'll wait in the car."

"Unless you think I can come in with you."

Dmitri got out of the car. I got out too. I realized too late he wished I would stay inside.

We walked up to a window you could tell was Plexiglas from the thick milky way it let the light through. There was heavy etching in the surface, like the cross-hatching I'd seen my artist friends do in their drawing classes. The design on this window was hazy, but it came together to spell out a discernible word: "Shit-head." A short woman approached the window. She saw Dmitri and a look of familiarity crossed her face. I couldn't understand their Russian. Dmitri took off the Orioles cap he was wearing and the change in his appearance was subtle but undeniable. His face looked as if it were a balloon puffed with two more breaths than when I'd seen him last. Under his right eye was a scalloped scar about the size and color of a pencil eraser.

The woman walked away from the window. She opened a door for us. We passed through a corridor into an office where a man was sitting behind a desk. He was short—even sitting down, I could tell he was about Dmitri's height and size and he wore silver rings on the first finger of each hand. A purple port-wine stain covered the lower half of the right side of his jaw and crawled down under the collar of his starched white shirt. He was the factory manager. The office reeked even more of the cherry smell that had struck me outside, and I began sneezing again.

The manager didn't look at me. Dmitri didn't bless me. My whole head was filled with the cloying smell, but neither Dmitri nor the manager seemed to notice it.

"So you would like to have this check for your mother," the manager said. Dmitri spoke back to him quickly in Russian.

"Slow, slow, Dmitri. I won't deny you anything," the manager said. "But you must speak to me in English if you want work." I hadn't detected his accent when the man first spoke, but now I could hear it in the yolky way he pronounced the word "anything."

"You will get it, here, here it is, read it." He held up the check so Dmitri could see the amount. The manager looked at me for the first time. His look dismissed my existence entirely. Dmitri winced.

"My mother says she has not been paid in two months," Dmitri said.

"And she is being paid now. Right now." He said it very sharply. Dmitri strained a smile. I watched the muscles at the base of his jaw work like there was a small rodent buried under his skin. Involuntarily, then, the skin of his nose, cheeks and forehead all rippled, the way a horse will flick the skin of its back to rid itself of flies.

"We thank you for it," Dmitri said. I could see that his eyes had welled up with water. He sat up straight, with his shoulders back. "And I cannot say thank you enough for offering me this opportunity. It is good."

Now the man behind the desk sat back again in his chair.

"You will be good, I'm sure," the manager said. "You will appreciate the opportunity you've been given, unlike some of these." The man waved his hand out as if to gesture after a group of ungrateful employees. Given that the only other person in the room was me, it appeared as if I was his example. He looked at me, realizing the implication. He wasn't embarrassed by it in the least. He looked back at Dmitri. Again, the skin around Dmitri's nose and cheeks twitched.

"Thank you," Dmitri said.

The two of us stood. The manager rose from behind the desk. When we reached the hallway—Dmitri and the man walked ahead of me, and I straggled behind, not wanting to come between them—Dmitri stopped. His new boss had been walking behind him, and now the man looked at Dmitri, as uncertain as I was why he wasn't moving forward. Then the man stepped in front of Dmitri into the room where the woman had let us in. Dmitri walked toward the exit only after the man did first.

*

After we left that place, Dmitri took me down to the basement of his house. He left me for a bit and I lit a cigarette. We didn't mention any of what happened in the factory on our ride home. I'd looked out the window and taken in my old town. Reisterstown Road had changed more than I had anticipated. There were three new strip malls opening where there had once been deep stands of trees, and where the businesses once gave way to farmland a billboard heralded the opening of a gated community called Wooded Oaks. But back in Greenhill, not much had changed—only Dimitri, and me, though I couldn't have said just yet how.

"So," I said. "You know I've been taking Russian Lit at school. They have us reading Dostoyevsky and Tolstoy." Dmitri didn't say anything. "I thought maybe you'd want to talk about some of those books."

"I don't care," Dmitri said. "What would you like, Samuel?" He hooked his thumbs in the loops on his jeans. A fecund smell wafted in from the flowerbeds just outside the window I'd cracked to smoke the cigarette.

"I guess to hear what it's been like for you," I said. "We haven't seen each other for so long."

"I meant, a drink or something."

"Oh. Water, I guess." Dmitri didn't move to get me anything.

"What do you want to know?"

"You're the one who emailed me."

"It's easy just to look someone up," Dmitri said. "Easier than being with them, Samuel."

"Sam."

"What?" Dmitri said.

"People all call me Sam now, not Samuel."

"Oĸ, Samuel," Dmitri said. The artificial cherry smell lifted off my clothing. Dmitri smelled it too, I could tell. His face betrayed the fact that he didn't know how to interact with this new version of me. Dmitri didn't have the same confidence, but he was just as obstinate as ever.

"I don't know what I want to know," I said. "I guess…What it was like in Hickey?"

"You don't want to know what it was like. There's nothing to tell."

"Oĸ," I said.

"I wasn't in Hickey the whole time," Dmitri said. "Before the trial I was in adult jail. They don't put you in with adults, like you think. You are alone in a cell for teenagers. After the hearing, I went to Hickey. I kept going back before Master Brown. Each time he hear about problems I had in there. Fights. Each time he didn't let me out."

He paused for a moment. A familiar flush came to his cheeks as he spoke. Seeing this Dmitri—the old Dmitri—made me feel suddenly that I was unchanged, too. A red so deep it was almost blue drew up into the scalloped scar under his right eye.

"I didn't get chance to get out like other kids. For two years I would be there and I see other kids come—the things some of them had done, the things they bragged about! I would not. I hated Goldstein, but I was not proud he was hurt. These other kids go before Master Brown and lie about their remorse and you never see them again."

His voice grew louder.

"I could not lie and say I had gotten better, say I was talking to a psychiatrist. Because of this they kept me. But I am no liar."

He stopped. It seemed he was waiting for me to say something.

"Your father made it over finally?" I said.

Until then, Dmitri had been speaking with his eyes trained to the floor. Now our eyes met. The high color blanched from Dmitri's face. The scar under his eye was again a fleshy pink.

"He is in Moscow," Dmitri said. He wasn't finished with telling me about his captivity, though. "After almost three years I finally go to another place called Cold Springs. It was not so much a detention center like Hickey. Instead there is outdoor education. Then this year when I come to my hearing there is a new Master. A woman. She asked how long I'd been there, and when I told her she said it was time for me to go home. She said I should have been back long time before. So now I am home."

It was the first time I'd ever heard him refer to Greenhill as home. Before this, home had always been Moscow.

"And now you're here, too," he said.

I fiddled with an unlit cigarette. Some dried tobacco flakes fell from its tip.

"You must have hated me so much all this time," I said.

"Hated you?" Dmitri leaned forward. "No one did anything for you. We hated Goldstein, and we went and did what we did. We did not think of the consequences. No one did anything because of you."

There was a prickly feeling all over my skin and face. I'd forgotten Dmitri—the way he spoke, the way he looked at you and hid nothing. Dmitri the sensualist.

"Do you have one?" he said. He was pointing at my cigarette.

We stood by the window and shared the cigarette. Dmitri took two drags, handed it to me. I could hear the dry leafy rustle of the burning ember at its tip. Things seemed quieter in that basement than when I was there last. I took two drags of the cigarette, handed it to him in that silence. It went on like that until it was done. We came back and sat on Dmitri's couch. We played *Super Mario*.

There was a large moon that early evening. I could see from the basement window where it hung up in the Baltimore sky. The Zilbers' basement was left with that dull tint rooms get just before dark, when everything has become grainy enough you can't quite make out even the chair across the room in its entirety, when the lines and details have grown imprecise enough it is as if the present moment has already faded into memory.

Our game ended. Dmitri turned on the light. I excused myself to the bathroom. While I was there I was gripped by a strange sensation.

"Do you know that feeling?" I said when I got out. "You know—the feeling you get when you're looking in a mirror and suddenly you see there's a hook to your nose you've never noticed, and suddenly you see your face as if for the first time?"

Dmitri looked me in the eyes. His lips drew taut. "No," he said.

He went back to his game.

I just hadn't described what I meant clearly enough. The feeling I was trying to convey, it's a feeling not unlike saying a word familiar to you over and over again like an incantation—Dmitri, Dmitri, Dmitri, Dmitri, Dmitri, Dmitri, Dmitri, Dmitri, Dmitri, Dmitri, Dmitri, Dmitri, Dmitri, Dmitri, Dmitri, Dmitri, Dmitri, Dmitri—so many times it loses its meaning, and gains a new one.

I joined Dmitri in a new game. Before he could decide to invite me to stay for dinner, or fail to, I told him I was going to take off for the Super 8 where I'd stayed the night before.

"I hope we can keep in touch," I said.

"We will," Dmitri said. It felt good to hear him say it, and I wished he'd stop there, but he didn't. "Or we won't. But we'll try."

I drove up the Beltway toward the highway home. As I drove, I realized for the first time something about that stretch of Beltway, something I hadn't noticed on my way down. I slowed to the speed limit. I looked until I realized what it was: all those sound barriers they were building through my final two years of high school were finally finished. They were brown, straight and tall, and they had been going up that last time I saw my grandfather before the burden of having outlived my grandmother—one last person he'd survived, one last idea he had about the vestige of his life before the war—led him to kill himself. They stood cordoning off all the neighborhoods that abutted the highway. Not just the wealthy developments, either. I'd gotten that wrong. They extended all the way to the city limits. That's what had quieted Dmitri's basement. Now that they were done, they didn't look so bad. In fact, it seemed as if they'd been there all along. They looked so natural, I couldn't even remember what it looked like before they were built.

*My immeasurable gratitude to:*

The mentors who walked me through early drafts of this story and suffered with me through all those clunky first drafts: Arthur Flowers, Mary Gaitskill, Amy Hempel, and George Saunders.

The embarrassingly long list of readers who provided notes over the many iterations of this story: Robin Black, Laura Farmer, Miciah Bay Gault, Tom Junod, Karl Kirchwey, Phil LaMarche, Adam Levin, Adrienne Miller, Jason Morris, Eric Rosenblum, Lauren Goodwin Slaughter, Thomas Yagoda—and the inimitably talented editor, Deena Drewis, who apparently came into this world blessed with a laser eye and ideas to burn.

James McClafferty at the Maryland Department of Juvenile Services, who opened the doors of the juvenile courts to me—without that experience I wouldn't have been able to make this happen. The Hungarian historian Randolph Braham, who gave to me his invaluable time and wisdom.

My mother and father, Barbara and John Torday, who plopped me down in Baltimore just long enough to have sufficient material for a novella, and my sister, Nicole Torday, who rode it out with us.

My grandparents, Steven Torday (1922–2011) and Maria Torday (1921–1994), who got out of Budapest and to the States with hope and luck, and who succeeded even when they didn't know to call it success.

And above all Erin and Abigail, who remind me every day why life and love are more important than books and words.